# DETECTIVE STORY

Imre Kertész

# Detective Story

TRANSLATED
FROM THE HUNGARIAN
BY

Tim Wilkinson

Harvill *Secker*
LONDON

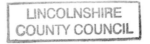
Published by Harvill Secker, 2008

2 4 6 8 10 9 7 5 3 1

First published with the title *Detekívtörténet*
by Magvető Könyvkiadó, Budapest 1977

First published in Great Britain in 2008 by
HARVILL SECKER
Random House
20 Vauxhall Bridge Road
London SW1V 2SA

Addresses for companies within The Random House Group Limited can be found at:
www.randomhouse.co.uk/offices.htm

The Random House Group Limited Reg. No. 954009
www.randomhouse.co.uk/harvillsecker

A CIP catalogue record for this book is available from the British Library

ISBN 9781846551833

Printed and bound in Germany by GGP Media GmbH, Pößneck

# Detective Story

# I

The manuscript that I am hereby making public was entrusted to my care by my client, Antonio R. Martens. As to who he is, you will learn that from him in due course. All that I shall say in advance is that, given his scholastic attainments, he evinced a surprising flair for writing, as indeed does anyone, in my experience, who for once in his life steels himself to face up to his fate.

I was appointed by the court as counsel for his defense. In the course of the criminal proceedings that were initiated against him, Martens did not try either to deny or to gloss over the charge against him of complicity in multiple murders. He did not fall into any of the behavioral categories with which the experience that I have gained to date in similar cases has made me familiar: either stubborn denial in respect to both material evidence and personal responsibility, or else that species of tearful remorse whose true motives are brutal unconcern for the victim and self-pity. On the contrary, Martens freely, readily, and uninhibitedly acknowledged his crimes as a matter of record—and with such stony indifference, it was as if he were giving an account of someone else's actions, not his own, those of another Martens with whom he was no longer to be identified, even though he was prepared to accept the consequences of his deeds without batting an eyelid. I considered him cynical in the extreme.

One day he turned to me with the surprising request that I secure the authorization needed for him to write in his cell.

"What do you wish to write about?" I asked him.

"About how I have grasped the logic," he replied.

"Now?" I was flabbergasted. "You mean you didn't understand it during your actions?"

"No," he replied. "Not during them. There was a time beforehand when I understood, and now I have understood again. During one's actions, though, one forgets. But then"—he gave a dismissive wave—"that's something people like you can't understand."

I understood better than he might have believed. All that surprised me was that I had not supposed that, with his being a lowly cog in a big machine and so having

4

relinquished all powers of discernment and appraisal of a sovereign human person, that person might stir again in Martens and demand his rights. That is to say, that he would wish to speak out and make sense of his fate. In my experience, that is the rarest case of all. And in my view, everyone has the right to do so, and to do it in his own way. Even Martens. So I set about securing what he requested.

Do not be surprised by his way with words. In Martens's eyes the world must have seemed like pulp fiction come true, with everything taking place in accordance with the monstrous certainty and dubious regularities of the unvarying dramatic form—or choreography, if you prefer—of a horror story. Let me add, not in his defense but merely for the sake of the truth, that this horror story was written not by Martens alone but by reality, too.

Martens finally handed the manuscript over to me. The text that is published here is authentic. I personally have not interfered with it in any way apart from making corrections where stylistic shortcomings absolutely demanded it. What he had to say, I have in all places left untouched.

## 2

I wish to tell a story. A simple story. You may ultimately
call it a sickening one, but that does not change its sim-
pleness. I wish therefore to tell a simple and sickening
story.

My name is Martens. Yes, the very same Antonio
Rojas Martens who is presently arraigned before the
judges of the new regime: the people's judges, as they
like to call themselves. You can read more than enough
about me these days, as the tub-thumping tabloids have
made sure that my name is known throughout Latin
America and maybe even over in distant Europe as well.

I must hurry, as most likely my time is short. It con-
cerns the Salinas case: Federigo and Enrique Salinas,
father and son, proprietors of the chain of department
stores that are dotted all over our country, whose deaths

so astounded people. Though back then people were not so easily astounded. But then no one believed that Salinas, whose name is given to the Uprising, could be a traitor. The Colonel did indeed later have cause to regret that we made news of Salinas's execution public; without a doubt it triggered a big moral backlash, far too big, and all quite unnecessarily. Still, if we had not issued a communiqué, then we would have been accused of seeking to mislead and of violating the law. Whatever we did, we were only ever going to get it wrong. The Colonel incidentally clearly saw that well in advance, and between you and me, so did I. But then what possible influence could a detective's beliefs have had on events here?

Back then I was still just a new boy with the Corps. I had transferred to them from the regular police, not from the political lot—they had long ago been taken over—but from the criminal investigation branch. "Hey, Martens!" says my boss one day. "Do you fancy a transfer?" "Where to?" I ask, being a cop, after all, and not a mind reader. He gave a toss of his head. "Over there," he says. "To the Corps." I said nothing, neither yes nor no. It wasn't bad in CID, but I was already starting to get a bit fed up with murderers, burglars, and whores. New winds were blowing, I had heard about one breakthrough and another, and there was said to be a future for anyone who made an effort. "The Corps is asking for men," the boss continued. "I was wondering whom I could recommend. You, Martens, have talent, and you'll be noticed sooner there."

Well, if you put it like that, I was thinking much the same myself.

I completed the course; they brainwashed me. Not enough, though, not by a long chalk. All sorts of things were still left in there, much more than I would have any need for, but then they were in a tearing hurry. Everything was screamingly urgent. Order had to be created, the Consolidation had to be pushed for, the Homeland saved, upheaval polished off; and it all seemed to come down to us. "We'll see about that," people would say if something were giving them a headache. I'm damned if I learned anything, but the work interested me. And the pay even more.

I ended up in Diaz's group (the Diaz for whom an APB has been put out, though to no purpose). There were three of us: Diaz, our boss (I can assure you all that he is never going to be found); Rodriguez (who has already been given a death sentence, just the once, though the scumbag deserves it a hundred times over); and myself, the new boy. Plus of course the auxiliary staff, cash, wide-ranging powers, and unlimited technology that your garden-variety flatfoot wouldn't even dare read about lest he get too carried away.

The Salinas affair soon intruded itself. Too early, damnably early. At precisely the time when my headaches happened to be at their worst. So it intruded, but nothing could be done about that; I have not been able to escape it since. I have to speak out, therefore, in order to leave behind some testimony before I go . . . before I am sent on my way. But forget that; it is the last thing on my mind right now. I was always set to do this. Our line of work is hazardous; once you get started, the only way back is to carry on straight ahead, as Diaz was in the habit of saying (you know: the one for whom an APB has been put out, though to no purpose).

Let me see, how did it start? And when? Only now that I am ordering my recollections do I have a sense of how hard it is to remember those early months of the Victory, and it's hard not just on account of the Salinases. Well, in any event we were already well past Victory Day, that's for sure, long, long past. The banners over the streets had gradually slackened and drooped, the slogans of the Victory on them were soaked through, the flags had wilted, and the street loudspeakers were hoarse from hammering out martial music.

Yes, that was how I saw it every morning when I crossed town to go from where I lived to the well-known classical palace where the Corps had set up operations. In the evenings I noticed none of this; no, in the evenings all I noticed was my headache.

Things were being made very uncomfortable for us around that time. The honeymoon period was over; the populace was getting jumpy. The Colonel too. On top of everything, we had picked up intelligence about an impending atrocity. We had to prevent that, or at least ought to have, with every available means: our Homeland and the Colonel demanded it of us.

That infernal jumpiness and the associated fluster were at the root of it all. Rodriguez was let loose, and Diaz—the ever-unruffled and ever-soothing Diaz— raised not so much as a peep against him. In point of fact, I had only then begun to see where I was and what I had taken on. As I say, I was still the new boy; up till then I had not done much more than loaf around. I was trying to figure out and enter into the spirit of things in order to be able to do what I had to do. I am an honest flatfoot, I always was, and I take my work seriously. Of course, I was aware that a different yardstick applied here at the Corps, but I thought there was at least a yardstick. Well, there wasn't, and that was when my headaches started.

Don't think I'm making excuses; for me it's now truly neither here nor there. But the fact is, you think you are being very clever in riding events out, and then you find that all you want to know is where the hell they are galloping off to with you.

That Rodriguez worried me most of all. He slowly became a mania with me. I wanted to be clear about him, figure him out, understand him like—yes, like Salinas his son perhaps. In another sense, of course, but with just the same investigative zeal. I say to him one day:

"Hey, Rodriguez, why are you doing that?"

"What?" he asks.

"Don't play the innocent with me, you bastard," I say sweetly. "Cut the *whats*!"

"Oh, *that*," he says, and smiles.

"Listen up," I continue. "We polish them off, crack down, roll up, interrogate—fair enough, that's our job. But why do you hate them?"

"Because they're Jews!" he snaps back. I was so astounded, I all but choked on my cigarette. I suspected that the book he was constantly concealing—it was in his hands right then—had driven him loopy. Was I supposed to believe that Rodriguez could speak English? He had to, since the book was in English, an American edition— one of those nasty contraband goods. There was no way of knowing how he had laid hands on it. Maybe he had confiscated it in the course of a house search. The only word that I understood from the garish title was "Ausch- witz," and that isn't an English word but the name of a place. I'd heard something about it, of course: it had been a long time ago and also a long way away, somewhere in that scummy Europe, in its eastern half. The hell if I could make out what it had to do with us, and how it entered into things.

"You crackpot!" I say to him. "There can't be more than a few hundred, or maybe a thousand, in the whole country."

"I couldn't care less," he says. "Anyone who wants something else is Jewish. Otherwise why would he want something else?" I just looked at him dumbfounded. Rodriguez had his logic, and no mistake. But once he had set off on the path of his logic, there was no stopping him. "Why?!" he bellowed in my face. "Why do they resist?"

"Because they're Jews." I tried to calm him down. I could see that his blood pressure was starting to rocket. I'd had enough of him. And then, however odd it may seem, what with me being a policeman, a member of the Corps—I was scared of him. His eyes smoldered. Rodriguez had the eyes of a leopard, only for heaven's sake don't look on that as any kind of compliment. It's just that, like those stinking big cats, he had yellow eyes with longish lashes.

My efforts to calm him down were in vain, however.

"Why do they resist?" He grabbed the shirt on my

chest. "We want what's good for them, we want to pluck them out of the filth. We want order for them, so we can be proud of them!" Oh yes, that's what he said: "so we can be proud of them." I was just thunderstruck.

"And yet they still don't want order." He kept on tugging at my shirt. "They're still resisting! Why? What for? Why?!"

A tricky question, indeed, as far as I was concerned. Seriously, why? I didn't know. I still don't know, not I. To be honest, I wasn't much interested either. I have never given any thought to motives; I've made do with the idea that there are criminals on the one hand and criminal investigators on the other. As far as I was concerned, I belonged to the latter category. In the CID that had been perfectly adequate; any speculations would have been a waste of energy. But with the Corpsmen, of course, it's different. There you need a philosophy, as Diaz put it, or a moral worldview, as they taught in the training course. I had neither: Rodriguez's view was not at all to my liking, whereas I didn't quite grasp Diaz's.

Maybe Diaz himself didn't take it seriously. With him you could never be sure. That sounds a little perplexing, what with Diaz being a serious man. Serious and deliberate, not at all the type cut out for wishful thinking. Once he happened to be leafing through some confiscated writings, the usual revolutionary tripe, a cigar clamped in one corner of his mouth, his inimitable smile in the other.

"Idiots!" He suddenly smacked the open palm of one hand down onto the document. "There's just one revolution that I can take seriously, and that's a police revolution!"

"Dern right!" Rodriguez concurred, with a guffaw.

"Idiot," Diaz said quietly to him. There was nothing strange about that; it was something he used to say. This time, however, he seemed angry—if Diaz could seem anything at all.

Another time—I no longer recall what prompted it—he declared out of the blue, "The world would look very different if we policemen were to stick together."

So I said, "But we do stick together, don't we?"

"Not just here, at home, but throughout the world!" he growled.

"In every state, you mean?"

"I do," says Diaz, elegantly crossing his legs, rocking his stocky, slightly squat upper body in his armchair, and shrouding his smooth, oily face in an enigmatic cloud of cigar smoke. It was getting into the afternoon; we were just taking a bit of a break, and the mood seemed cordial. At such times, it does one good to chat, even with the boss.

So I dug a little further. "You mean the police of hostile states as well?"

At that he raised a finger. "Nowhere and at no time," he said, "are the police hostile."

I was unable to drag anything more out of him, though, however nice the afternoon.

When all's said and done, I don't know if he genuinely believed this view. Today I'm inclined to suppose that he did. A person has to believe in something to be such a nasty piece of work. In any event, he would often come back to the subject, never entirely seriously, always in that ambivalent way he had, but I wouldn't be a policeman if I didn't know what that means.

It's just that it was of precious little help to me. There is no denying that by then more than once I had caught myself stuttering. Then at other times I would drop into my speech stupid expressions like "thingy" and "I mean" and "how should I put it" and suchlike that previously I had never been in the habit of using. And a good job too! Just imagine, a policeman who stutters, jiggles uneasily with his hands, and trails off in the middle of sentences. I quickly kicked the habit; by then my headaches were plenty for me to put up with.


Anyway, it soon became clear what Rodriguez had picked up from that book. One fine day a statuette appeared on his desk. It was small, some four to six inches high, no bigger than a paperweight, but you could still see everything, clearly and distinctly. Rodriguez kept that statuette on his desk all the time. Before long a copy of it was also ready, and this was no longer a model but life-size, roughly five feet tall. Rodriguez had his assistant install it in the room next door. He had found that chap for himself, among the lower ranks, and I have to say he chose well: anyone who took one look into that ape face could have no doubt, and no mistake. Otherwise he was silent as a shark and as eager as a trained gorilla. His military blouse was forever unbuttoned at the neck, his sleeves were rolled up to the elbow on his hairy arms, and he reeked of sweat and liquor and filth of every kind. That room was their kingdom—"my operating theater" as Rodriguez called it.

I'm reluctant to talk about it, but it can't be avoided. I'm damned if it's of any interest to me; it never was. But now they keep asking me about it—the examining magistrates, that is. It's useless my declaring I gave even the vicinity of that lousy room a wide berth. "So," one of them will pipe up from the rostrum, "you claim that you were unaware of what was going on in the room known as the operating theater?" The hell I'm claiming! "All I said, sir, was that I didn't drop by the room." "I see," he gloats triumphantly. "And what do you have to say about the statement made by witness Quintieros that he saw you in the so-called operating theater on several occasions?" Well, if your witness saw it, then obviously that's how it was. What cleverdicks! As if I cared in the slightest whether I dropped by the room or not. But then what do I expect, magnanimity? At least I'm allowed to write in my cell—that's something we would never have permitted. It went against all the rules.

So as I said, this statue appeared on Rodriguez's desk. It was made for him by a sculptor from down below: there were prisoners of every kind in our jails, so why not a sculptor? This sculptor, by the way, was not a genuine sculptor but a monument mason. Still, he did a good job, I'll say that for him. He made it of wood and some kind of plastic, if I'm not mistaken. It consisted of a base on which stood two uprights ending in forks. Resting on the forks was a rod, which in turn supported a tiny human figure in such a way that it passed between the bent knees and the wrists handcuffed together behind the knees. A devastating contraption, no two ways about it. Diaz glowered at it.

"What on earth is that?" he asked.

"That? It's a Boger swing," Rodriguez responded with great affection.

"Boger?" Diaz fussed. "What do you mean, Boger?"

"That's the name of the fellow who invented it," Rodriguez explained. He flicked the diminutive doll on the head with an index finger. It spun a few times, then the momentum died down, and it just swung on the rod, head down. You could see the thighs and the crudely carved buttocks, not omitting what lies in between. To Rodriguez's credit, it should be made clear that it was a male doll.

"This bit here"—Rodriguez traced a small circle over it with his finger—"is freed up. You can do with him what you will." He looked up at Diaz and grinned. I might as well not have been there—which is just as well as I probably only would have stuttered. That reflects badly on a person. "Or else," Rodriguez continued, "you can squat down here, by his mug, and ask him whatever you want to know."

Diaz hemmed and hawed. He strode up and down the room a couple of times, hands clasped behind him. That was his habit when he was mulling something over, or if something was not to his liking. The day he made his getaway he did that for the entire morning, until in the end I felt dizzy.

He perched one buttock on Rodriguez's desk.

"What in the blue blazes do you need it for?" he inquired in a fatherly tone. "We've got every sort of plaything. All you have to do is press a button, and it switches on an electric current. That's what they use the world over these days: clean and convenient. Isn't that enough for you?"

No, it wasn't enough. Rodriguez didn't believe in mechanization.

"A person," he says, "has no direct contact."

"What's that to you?" Diaz asked.

He failed to convince Rodriguez, however, who had his own principles. An educated man was Rodriguez; he would follow up on anything that interested him. "It's too fiddly with machines," he says. "Pure mechanics. One might as well don a white gown, like an engineer or surgeon. There's no more interaction than if one were handling the matter by telephone. The offender can't see the good humor one is in. And yet," so Rodriguez, "that's the key to the effect."

As I said, I'm reluctant to talk about this. Even then I had nothing to say—I was still a new boy, and then again I was nervous about the stuttering and the clichés. I told Diaz what I thought only after Rodriguez had left the room to attend to business, as the workmen were by then already erecting the frame.

"Swine!" I said.

"That he is," Diaz nodded with feeling, abstractedly twirling the doll. "A swine. A rat. A bloodsucker."

He fell silent. Neither of us said a word. Even that poxy doll was by then dangling motionless between us, head downward.

"And you." All at once he lifted his eyes to look at me. "What are you so windy about, sonny boy?" Diaz could have a very disagreeable way of looking at you, though he had tranquil, dark brown eyes and did nothing to alter that. I mean, he did not narrow them or glower or stare—he just looked, nothing more. But that was disagreeable all the same.

"Me?" I retort. "Not windy, absolutely not. Just thingy . . . that's taking it a bit too far."

"Too far indeed, too far." He nods. "Well, we have dealings with the far out."

"Sure, sure," says I. "It's just . . . how should I put it . . . I mean, I actually thought we were serving the law here."

"Those in power, sonny boy," Diaz corrects me. My head started to ache. Oddly, it was actually Diaz who made it ache, not Rodriguez.

To that I say, "Up till now I thought the two were the same."

"Fair enough," Diaz concedes. "Only you shouldn't lose sight of the order."

"What order is that?"

"Those in power first, then the law," Diaz says quietly with that inimitable smile of his.

So, that was how matters stood when we had to decide whether to arrest Enrique Salinas or simply put him under surveillance.

No.

Events are now getting muddled and snarled together in my brain: the strands of the investigation that I, as investigating officer, held in my hands; the interrogations; Enrique's diary; the lengthy chats that I had as ostensibly supplementary interrogations with him and his father, the elder Salinas, that utterly determined old fox; the tape recordings of the conversations they had with each other in prison; and finally my own unformulated thoughts about it all, which have subsequently confused the case in my mind so thoroughly that speaking about it will prove harder, I fear, than I suspected at first.

At that time we had done nothing more than open a file on Enrique. We already knew about him. He featured in the records as an abstract piece of data, and we knew that sooner or later he would have to play a part in person. We didn't speak about it: there was nothing to say, but we just knew. We waited patiently, without even thinking that we were waiting; as I have said, we had a lot to do at the time. We had an atrocity to prevent. Whether his case would fall within the scope of the case set in motion by the atrocity, or of some other case, we truly couldn't have cared less. Any person who was in the records was going to end up as a suspect sooner or later, no question. That's as sure as the fact that I am sitting and writing in my cell here, until . . . But let's drop that subject. The sentence has not been handed down yet, and even when it is, I shall be granted a short time afterward, at least until an appeal is heard. I know how it goes in this sort of case.

In short, our records had already identified that Enrique was going to perpetrate something sooner or later. As far as we were concerned, his fate was sealed, even if he himself had not yet made up his mind. He was hesitating, playing for time. He roamed the streets or wrote in his diary, raced around in his Alfa Romeo, visited on friends, or popped into bed with some silky-smooth kitten, if he happened to feel so inclined. Enrique Salinas was young, just twenty-two; his long hair, his wisp of a mustache and beard alone marked him as suspicious in our eyes. He brooded, rushed around, and made love. He did not spend much time at home. Maria, for her part, sat by the window and waited for him. Not that she could have seen much from the eighteenth floor of the Salinas luxury apartment building. From up there the milling bustle of the Grand Boulevard looks like the teeming of ants. Nevertheless, Maria Salinas, Enrique's mother, spent all her time by the window.

That was where old Federigo Salinas found her when, on returning from the office, he crossed the apartment's opulent salons in search of his wife. He stood behind her back without uttering a word.

"I'm scared," he hears Maria say after a while.

"We have no reason to be scared, Maria," he retorts. They fall silent.

"Hernandez has disappeared. Martino has been executed. Vera was taken away from her home," Maria recites without even turning around.

"We're not the kind of people they take away." Salinas put an arm around her shoulders.

Maria was somewhat comforted. A sense of strength emanated from Salinas's arm. Strength, superiority, and certainty. Slippery as an eel was old Salinas, though one should not picture him as being old: he looked young for his age. He was fifty, in the prime of life in certain respects.

"Look!" he hears Maria's agitated voice again. "Federigo, look down there!" She was pointing at the street. He could see a black limousine. It was one of the vehicles that belong to our department—from time to time we had a job to do on the Grand Boulevard.

"Come away from the window, Maria!" Salinas spoke firmly to her.

Don't go thinking I am just making up these exchanges. I wasn't there, of course, how could I have been? But they have passed through my hands. I have seen them and heard them, watched them and interrogated them. I made records of what they said, to the point that all at once the records began to take charge of me.

We interrogated Maria as well—most certainly I interrogated her. That was at Diaz's express request, incidentally. I objected, because I saw no point. Diaz, however, insisted. So I interrogated her. I interrogated her once, and then again on several further occasions, as Diaz wished. Maria was an attractive woman, slim, trim, and elegant. She had left her dark hair undyed, with good reason: the few gleaming silver strands only heightened its sheen. She was forty-eight, and it was still possible to fall head over heels in love with her, you bet! Those eyes! I was glued to them like a fly to flypaper. Sometimes I almost felt as if she were interrogating me, and not the other way around. But then I would notice the fear in those eyes, and that would at least restore order between us, even if I was unable to fully regain my composure. No, if a woman like that is afraid, that is alarming.

We were not going to be able to learn anything from her—all of us were clear about that. I have no liking for senseless work, and I said as much to Diaz, as I have already mentioned.

What I said to him was:

"There's no sense in this. If it were up to me, I'd leave the woman out of the case."

"That's not possible. Besides, she would be offended," he brushed me off. A helluva witty guy Diaz could be. At the time I just put that remark too down to his wit, but then things turned out differently. As I say, I was the new boy, and I was not yet in a position to appreciate all the subtleties of our work. Maria Salinas had to survive so as to grieve and bring us into disrepute. No one was left without a role in this game, and that was her role. So we handled her with kid gloves. She underwent formal interrogations, with polite questions and tactful expectations. These were more in the line of visits to a clinic, with a tidy transcript attesting to each of them. That sort of thing is important as proof of the impeccable legality of our procedures.

With Salinas I was able to speak more freely. Over time, once we were able to regard his case as closed, I managed to gain his trust. Later he even came to welcome the chats. That's understandable, since he was then able to bring up all the things he had ever been fond of. He was thereby able to relive the various episodes of his life and ponder his misfortune. I, for my part, was able to forget who I was supposed to be (the case was closed, after all) and, as a faithful witness, listened to him like some kind of reverential pupil.

So I am very well aware what they talked about, better than if I had been there in person.

"Federigo . . . how long can this go on?" Maria asked.

"The name says it all: a state of emergency," said Salinas. He was getting a bit bored with the matter. He had already said it all a hundred times over, but he'd say it another hundred times if necessary. He lit a cigarette. Salinas smoked fragrant cigarettes—a stylish brand, in this as in everything. That was something in which he could indulge himself, that's for sure.

"Not long, then?" Maria badgered him some more, but this time she got no answer. "It won't be for long?" she pressed him. "Not for long, Federigo, will it?"

"No," Salinas reassured her. "It's always like this. I can give you any number of examples. They come and they go; the worse they are, the quicker." He paused. "One only has to get through it. And we have every chance of doing that, Maria," he finished off with a smile.

A nice line, for domestic consumption, and Salinas had by now carefully polished every detail. Maria knew the follow-up herself:

"Provided we stay outside both circles," she said, as if intoning it.

"That's right." He nodded staunchly. "That of the persecutors and that of the persecuted."

"Is it that simple, Federigo?" she inquired. The query was unexpected and was not in keeping with the rules of the game. Salinas shot a quick, suspicious glance at his wife. He had to think.

"No," came the cautious reply. "Obviously, the circles are expanding all the time."

"Like the eddies of a whirlpool," she said.

"If you like," he gracefully conceded. He waited. Nothing happened. Maria contented herself with the simile. Salinas could relax. "It's all a matter of timing," he remarked.

"And the pace of events," she said.

"Naturally." He nodded. They had again sorted out their differences. That was how they played the game nowadays, every evening: a delicate game it was, requiring them to heed the rules.

"I'm suffocating!" Maria said unexpectedly.

"No, just choking," Salinas comforted her. "As am I, as is everybody." He suddenly became nervous, this time genuinely nervous. "Don't look at your watch," he entreated his wife. "He'll be back home."

They then fell silent. Each sank into an armchair. Salinas blew fragrant smoke rings. He stretched out his long, muscular legs, his black patent-leather shoes gleaming in the twilight. He undid the buttons of his impeccable suit jacket and loosened his fashionable necktie.

Maria was sitting with a straight back, hands resting in her lap.

They waited. They were waiting for Enrique, both of them—for the Enrique whom we had already entered into our records and for whom they were anxiously longing as for their destiny.

.  .  .

Enrique's diary lies before me. I am leafing through it. I have long ago cracked his in-places-indecipherable lines; I'm familiar with their content. The diary was confiscated in the course of a house search, and I purchased it after Enrique's death. I have brought it with me even in here. No particular difficulties were raised; I told them I would like to write my memoirs, and I needed the notebook for that. They went through it, as is only proper, but then handed it over. I have it really soft in here, I can't complain. There's no two ways about it: with us, requests like that were unlikely to have been honored, as the wiseguys who make the rules are in the habit of phrasing it. I told them that it was my diary, and in a sense I wasn't lying: after all, I had bought it.

It's good that I have it with me. It was smart of me to buy it. Even now I don't know what on earth possessed me to do that. I acquired it simply because I felt it couldn't possibly end up anywhere else; it had to be with me. So I purchased it from the head of our confidential archives, who handles deposited documents of this sort. I readily came to an understanding with him, because I knew his weakness, and it so happened I could be of assistance to him in the matter. In the matter of certain top-notch brands of liquor. At the time shortages had sprung up as a result of humdrum disputes about reciprocal customs tariffs and foreign-exchange considerations—no doubt you all recall those dry months. He didn't want a lot: I would have been willing to put up even five times as much for Enrique's diary. Fortunately, he wasn't to know that. He then did the necessary paperwork.

Surprised, are you? Why? I can tell much stranger tales than that one. If I were to get going, there'd be no end to them—all manner of things happened in our setup. After all, the people working for the Corps are only human. People everywhere are only human, and of all sorts, what is more.

Enrique began keeping the diary when the university was closed. After Victory Day, in other words.

Opening it at random:

> To give an account of my days is impossible. To give an account of my plans: I have none. To give an account of my life: I'm not living.
> They have smashed my hopes, smashed my future, smashed everything, the scum!

Leafing further on:

> I exist. Is this a life still? No, just vegetating.
> It seems that only one philosophy can
> succeed the philosophy of existentialism:

nonexistentialism, the philosophy of nonexistent existence.

That, I have to confess, is a little over my head. I know nothing about philosophy. It may sound odd, but sometimes I have the same trouble with Enrique as I do with Diaz: I can't follow him. He too gave me a headache—a different sort of headache, of course, utterly different.

I turn the page:

Nonexistence. The society of the nonexistent. In the street yesterday a nonexistent person trod on my foot with his nonexistent foot.

I took a stroll in the city. It was infernally hot. The usual evening hubbub around me. Lovers on the pavements, hurrying to cinemas and other places of amusement as if nothing had happened, nothing. Living their nonexistent lives. Or do they exist, and it's me who doesn't? Every other guy in the street seemed to have lost something. There are these police types everywhere, eavesdropping, sniffing around, and they think nobody is paying any attention to them. They're right too: people don't pay them any attention. All it has taken is a few months, and already they have grown accustomed to them.

I dropped in on a café, flopped down on the
terrace. I was boiling with anger, the heat, and
impotence. A packed terrace, a waxwork gallery of
the petty bourgeoisie. People chattering on about
business, fashion, and entertainment. One woman
was cackling interminably in a shrill voice. The
perfumes of the ladies mingled with the soft,
glutinous smell of bloated, greasy bodies. To my
right was a swarthy fellow, his oily, short-cropped
black hair combed back in the American style, his
chubby cheeks swollen at the base of the ears as if
he had mumps, and he was wearing black-rimmed
spectacles. His lips were continually in motion and
smacking, as if he were talking to himself or
sucking a sweet. But then I noticed that he was
trying to achieve a compromise, a modus vivendi,
with an oversize set of dentures. He had his wife
with him, a faded beauty. They were joined later
on by a bald guy, likewise with his wife, and a drab
young man who was evidently Baldy's son. I
shamelessly eavesdropped. The son considered it
timely to remark that it had been a hot day, to
which False Teeth responded: "Never mind what
it was like. The main thing is we've got through
it." Then he unexpectedly declared: "In any case,
we all check out six feet under." I jerked up my
head in astonishment: could he possibly be aware

of where he was living? But no, I satisfied myself that it was only the choppers that had made him such a skeptic. The lower and upper rows of teeth were like two camel's hooves (though come to think of it, camels don't have hooves) that had been crammed into his mouth in an absurd and mad fit, and now he had to go around with them forever, out of some sense of obstinacy and grim determination. His wife, the faded beauty, babbled on incessantly in an effortlessly prissy voice. She joyfully reported that a new consignment was in, and listed all the things that could now be obtained at the market. Baldy's wife also chimed in, then Baldy himself. They agreed that life was getting better as the consolidation was taking hold. They were pleased to establish that distinct signs of life were detectable in the business sphere. Conditions were improving—that was Baldy's view. A mood of optimism sprang up. They ordered another round of refreshers. With the greatest of pleasure I would have tossed a bomb among them.

Turning the page:

It's not been possible to talk to the guys since the university was closed on account of the ructions. I know they're up to something, though; I know they meet somewhere. I went out to the beach on the Blue Coast. There they were; I knew it. I tried to speak with C., but he laughed it off. He said they had come out to have a swim. They don't trust me. It's all because of my father, simply because I'm his son and I happened to be born into his fortune. Excluded from everywhere. How humiliating!

Turning the page:

The idea of suicide surfaces, regular as clockwork, as the evening draws in. That is when it is the most alluring. As the sun goes down, a woman's seductive power, and like some tropical sap it gets under my skin, softens up my muscles, loosens the innards, draws my head toward my guts, thaws the bones, fills me with a sickly-sweet disgust, to give in to which is a nauseating pleasure. One thing I can direct against it is my uneasy love for my mother.

Then too the lack of means. Father's revolver: but he keeps that in the safe. I let slip the chance to acquire one of my own; of late it has become fairly difficult. Yet that's the most advantageous on account of its practicality, its cleanness, and the unutterably simple blast, after which I imagine there would be a profound stillness, then nothing more. Everything else involves work and fuss. Hanging: having to choose a rope and a good place on the ceiling, then tying the noose and trying it out—not to speak of having to kick the chair away from under one! Then the cracking— and here I can't shrug off the spectacle, the inevitable lack of consideration that I would be showing to those I love. My poor mother! . . . Or jumping out onto the Grand Boulevard. But then the fall, the time it would take before hitting the ground, the sight of the asphalt rushing up to my eyes with a single jolt, and then the scream! Drugs sicken me.

Of course, living is another way of killing oneself: its drawback is that it takes so horribly long.

Turning the page:

> Under certain circumstances suicide is not acceptable. It shows a lack of respect for the wretched, so to say.

Is that so? Something about these lines, I must admit, always brings a prickle to my eyes. Enrique was still young, very young. He had to have a reason for everything, even for living. That type is still a child, not yet a fully grown man. All the same, on account of lines like that I felt it was intolerable that Enrique's diary should lie moldering in some archive. Even now it is a solace to me that I purchased it.

Turning the page:

> I've had a bellyful of my life. Break with this inaction, emerge from the stillness! . . . Yes, muteness is truth; but a truth that is mute, and the ones who speak will be right.
>
> I have to speak. More: to act. To make an attempt at leading a life that I shall try to make worth the trouble of living it.

Turning the page:

> The accident yesterday: before my eyes a white automobile slammed into a motorbike rider. The shriek. The female pillion passenger was laid out by the curb. People stood around. Her blood slowly puddled on the roadway.
>
> This morning the lame woman who sells newspapers . . . She has a daughter, a delightful child, quite clearly the newspaper woman's only

hope in life. She spends more than she can afford on clothing her, showers her with sweets. This morning the little girl ran away from her and came to a stop farther off in the traffic. The mother called, in vain: the girl teased her from afar, thumbing her nose, pulling faces. The lame newspaper woman kept coaxing her: "Come here, my child, there's a nice girl. Eat your chocolate!" Finally the child sidled up to her. As soon as she was within reach, the newspaper woman grabbed her and started hitting her—with the tenacity of the wretched and the mercilessness of those who have had their hopes made a mockery of.

I am sick of atrocities, though these are now the natural order of our world. And I would still like to act!

Leafing on:

I met R. in the street.

Leafing on:

I had a chat with R. A possible friendship? Odd that at university we hardly noticed each other.

Leafing on:

R. came over. He confessed that at the
university he hated me, taking me for a rich and
carefree playboy. We had a good laugh. R. is poor.
He has been attending university on a scholarship
and has to work during the vacations. We then
both spoke our minds. He thinks the same way
about it all as me, but his bitterness is even more
extreme—maybe even a touch too much. But then
that is understandable, as he is making a bigger
sacrifice to study, and now everything seems to be
in vain. He admitted that he is very scared. He is
constantly haunted by that feeling, yet he is ready
for anything. It's curious: I'm not afraid, yet I am
cautious all the same. He says he must do
something: true, it may not free him from his fear,
but it would tie him to something for good. I asked
him if he was planning anything, or maybe was
already working for certain somebodies. (The
stupid expressions that one finds oneself getting
into!) He did not give a definite answer but
smiled ambiguously. He too does not trust me.
It rankled me.

R. was not much to Mother's liking,
incidentally. I asked her why. "He has strange

eyes," she said. What kind of reason is that! I had a good laugh and kissed her.

Leafing on:

> R. came by. I told him that I might possibly be game to take part in something that made sense. He promised nothing. All the same, I somehow felt relieved to have finally broken my oppressive silence and caution. Now at least someone knows about me: I am no longer so much on my own. I must win his confidence. I am sure he is up to something.

I shall stop for now. I'm closing the diary. I'm sitting and musing—musing about Enrique, that child who was so thirsty for life, action, friendship, and love.

And I'm musing about R., in whom he sensed an unexpected possibility of friendship.

By then we were already well acquainted with R. He was Ramón; Maria's remark precluded any other possibility. It was Ramón, yes: Ramón G., also known as Steeleyes.

How should I characterize him? Imagine, if you will, a leech, but a leech that is capable of ardor—and there you have Ramón. He was always sucking someone's blood, tenaciously, persistently, devotedly. He had a special talent for making people talk. Damned if I know how he did it. But anyone he sank his sucker into started speaking almost immediately, as if some kind of serum had been inoculated into their body, along with his saliva. Guys like him seem to have one ploy: they somehow manage to arouse a person's interest—then they immediately clam up. From then on they just keep quiet. Oh, and they always have time, of course. Those types look like lost souls who can be saved only by the victims, with their small talk and their advice, often with their money and, sometimes, their body. In regard to the latter, as far as Ramón was concerned it was just about the same to him whether it was a woman or a man. Indeed, he had a particular partiality for both at once, though it would be wrong to say that he insisted on that at any price. Ramón was modest and always had a feel for opportunities. When he had got his fill of someone's blood, he would detach himself from that person and attach himself to another. At these times, however, he would recall the savor of all his previous prey, and the new victim would nearly always be delighted to learn that Ramón's circle of acquaintances—which in each and every case would partly overlap with theirs—consisted of cretins, moral deadbeats, or contemptible lowlifes. Then the victims would gush words to present the opposite picture of themselves. Ramón would keep quiet. He encouraged them with his silence, egged them on with his understanding, tickled them with his humility or his admiration, set them on a pedestal above himself through his own abasement. And he would observe this victim, fixing his stern, totally reflective, lifeless, and slightly crazed eyes with greedy attentiveness on his victim, while his mind meanwhile was already working on the next.

Ramón was a good-looking young man, tall, gaunt, with dark hair, who looked good in the casual sportswear in which he was usually clothed.

It was just his eyes that Maria found strange. The Corps' narcotics experts would have conferred on them a more accurate term. At the time, that sort of thing was taken seriously—the Homeland's moral subsistence rested on the Corps' conscience. The Colonel placed great stress on that, wanting to see a clean people and clean souls. This was among the exceptional pronouncements that he would utter, with exactly the same emphasis, both in parliament and in the Corps' premises. So on a few occasions we cracked down here and there. The price of drugs would go up. Ramón right then was left without a supply, and his eyes were even duller, even more steely-gray and vacant as a result. All he was left with were slander, fear, clearsightedness, and resentment.

Everything Ramón told Enrique was true. He had

won a scholarship, he did have to work in his vacations, he was poor. By the way, he was not poor because his parents were poor: he had run away from home when he was seventeen. The devil knows how he managed not to acquire a criminal record, but we still knew about the things that were of interest to us. He ran off with Max, a well-known homosexual, who when filling out a form, in the space for occupation would write "philosopher." Ramón then split up with Max and bummed around. He joined a commune that produced craft goods: they wove and sewed, a mix of men and women—in the nude. I'll be damned if I know what the fun is in that. He left the commune and took up with a girl. He left the girl and took up with a woman who was ten years older. He left her . . . I won't continue. A restless spirit was Ramón, as you can see. He was looking for solid ground under his feet because he was afraid, afraid of himself and everybody else. He was afraid of society because—so he says—he is familiar with its murderous laws. And he was afraid of the police above all; he feared and loathed them. But if you want my opinion, Ramón simply needed fear, God knows why. Don't look to me for explanations; I know nothing about what makes the mind tick. I'm just a flatfoot, that's the profession I trained for. What I can say, though, is that a guy like him was not exactly a big deal for us. We have more than enough of his type. They fear in order to be able to loosen up suddenly. They view everybody and everything as sordid so as to become sordid themselves. Apart from that, each of them individually is different.

Meanwhile this Ramón was attending the university. People there suspected almost nothing. He passed his examinations with flying colors. His knowledge earned him respect. His manner deceived his professors; he listened to them, and they talked to him. It was just his eyes . . . but then I have already touched on that. So, add it all up—that's what kind of person Ramón was.

He fell into our hands by pure chance. That is to say, it was pure chance that he fell into our hands right then. It could easily have been any other time, but I have no doubt that sooner or later, whatever happened, he was going to fall into our hands. In this case, the occasion was offered by what Enrique's diary refers to as "the ructions at the university."

As ructions go, these ones were not such a big deal. We hauled in a few kids, but no one paid much attention. It was soon after Victory Day, and every prison and holding cell was packed, the detainees were crammed together in corridors like sardines. We were not given much time to clarify the workings of university democracy. A smack or two here and there, and Diaz would summarily release the bulk of them. His eye alighted on

Ramón, however, and he had him stand up in the corridor, forehead and palms of the hands to the wall, as you're supposed to do.

The day before we had worked through the night; I was fed up with the kids by then.

"What do you want from him?" I asked Diaz.

"I don't know," he replied. Diaz was indefatigable, and he had an infallible eye. We knew nothing about Ramón, except that he had no priors, which we learned over the telephone. Otherwise, nothing. It was still the early days, the Victory was still fresh, the records were as yet deficient. Tracking down an identity would take days. Diaz was in a hurry. We had things to do.

So he called him in from the corridor and sat him down. He fired a few questions at him, purely at random. Ramón held his ground well, but Diaz knew how to ask questions. About a quarter of an hour later Ramón started yelling. He couldn't bear the tension any longer. When he told Enrique that he had to do something that would tie him to something for good, he hadn't been lying. He was lucky that an eye had happened to spot this about him. And Diaz loved helping those in need.

As I say, Ramón started yelling. He dumped all his hatred on our heads. It was like someone throwing up. He called us character assassins, spinning nets to catch the innocent. Butchers, murderers, hangmen, and so on. Diaz listened with bowed head, elbows on the desk, hands covering his face. He was taking a breather. Then all of a sudden Ramón fell silent. Stillness descended, a long stillness. Diaz then got ponderously to his feet. He slowly made his way around, then popped one buttock on the front of the desk. His preferred position. He sat like that for a while, facing Ramón, then suddenly leaned forward. He didn't overstrain himself, and took care not to leave any lasting marks. Rodriguez followed suit. Me being the new boy, I took down a record of the interrogation.

After that it wasn't necessary to say a lot. Ramón took his seat again, and Diaz asked if he smoked. He did. Diaz offered him his cigar case. Rodriguez asked if he was thirsty. He was. Rodriguez set a glass before him and took the orange juice from the refrigerator. (We drank that deuced orange juice all day long on, amid all that diabolical work and heat.)

Diaz then briefly outlined what Ramón had to do, at what intervals, and through whom, and he explained in what form he was to make his reports.

It was from him that we first heard the name of Enrique Salinas.

I have to admit that up to this point I have skipped over some pages of Enrique's diary. That was not a good idea. They tell an important strand in the story line leading to the fateful auto drive, so it was not clever of me to omit them.

Nor was it fair. But I am seeking to be fair: when better than now for me to be honest. Fair to Enrique, first and foremost, but also fair to Estella and to myself as well.

Let me leaf back through the pages, back almost to the beginning of Enrique's diary.

That a mouth could have the shape (and
movements) of a flower (a flower in a breeze) is
quite incredible. And yet there is such a mouth.

I leaf further on: an empty page with just two letters on it:

E.J.

Estella Jill, or simply Jill. He preferred to use her second, English name. She was American on her mother's side. Turning the page:

J. Like someone in whom the sun shines inside.
I sunbathed the whole afternoon.

Yes, that too is Enrique's voice. Suicidal thoughts, confused street scenes, self-encouragement, hatred, and love. And all of it side by side, knotted together, jumbled up. Enrique was an adolescent, a child.

I'm turning the pages. I leaf quite a bit further on, and then quite out of the blue:

How did it happen? I don't know. All of a sudden I was holding her in my arms. I locked the door. I leaned over her, sank my mouth between her lips. We lay on the couch's thick, Indian-weave blanket. We were naked and snuggled up to each other. I sensed that she desired me. Then a dreadful, stupid, and inexplicable thing happened. I have to write it down. The only way I shall shake it off is by writing it down. Yet even now I am overwhelmed by the hideous and, at the same time, ludicrous ordeal of those long, long minutes.

Out with it! In short, I couldn't respond to her desire—me, who had been waiting for this very moment for weeks! I just lay beside her, impotent. She embraced me. I could feel her trembling. Then the trembling passed. She just caressed me with a now cool hand, like a nursery schoolteacher. I didn't dare look at her. Then she spoke. She said she was grateful to me. I could have taken her, made her my own, but it was her I wanted, not the opportunity and chance. She would never forget that, she said. She

snuggled up contentedly—her body was cool by
then—and kissed me, on both eyes and my brow.
Then she got up and started to dress, meanwhile
looking at me all the time and smiling. I reached
out for her. She sat down beside me, at the edge
of the couch. Now it was she who leaned over
me. She started to caress me. Such a light and soft
touch! She stroked me until . . . Then she again
discarded her underwear. Very slowly and
deliberately, meanwhile looking at me and smiling.
I almost lost my senses! Finally, she lay down
beside me. And then . . .

Later on we went out to a bar. We laughed the
whole evening, laughed and laughed!

I turn the page:

Happiness makes you lose your mind. That
doesn't matter, but then happiness paralyzes you.
I forget about everything else. I'm living as if I
had a right to live; I'm living as if I were really
existing. I make plans, dream of the future, build
a life for the two of us, want to marry her—as
though no one else but us were alive. Meanwhile
I sense how absurd this all is, as there is no future,
only the present, a state, a state of emergency.

I turn the page:

> I talked it over with her. I let her know what I
> am thinking. She understood; she agreed on every
> point. I felt inexpressible gratitude and relief. I
> gripped her hand. And then all of a sudden she
> began talking about the wedding and how we
> would furnish the home.

I turn the page:

> I can't stand it anymore. I'm an idiot; I myself
> don't know what I want. I have to decide finally:
> her or . . . And what about both? No, that's
> impossible . . . But nevertheless, what if? . . . I
> can't see clearly; the trouble is that I don't see
> clearly. In point of fact, I am now beginning to
> grasp—dreadful feeling—that I don't really know
> her. And not just her but myself, or at least not
> enough. I have to know what I want. I have to get
> to know both her and myself. But how? Talking is
> not enough; words don't clarify anything. I'll have
> to hit upon something, but what?

He hit upon driving.

So I'll have to describe that car trip. Not that it will be

difficult, as I am familiar with every detail. Enrique put down an outline in the diary, but I also spoke to him in person about it. Whatever gaps were still left, Estella filled in, or rather let's stay with just Jill.

We interviewed her too at the time. We didn't make much use of her. We accepted her statement that she had been embroiled in the case unsuspectingly. So that was how it went: we didn't look to Jill for anything. But then order is order. A transcript has to be made of everything. In this case we could again point to a transcript, which again merely corroborated the all-embracing thoroughness of our investigations and their impartiality.

I felt a sort of respect for Enrique at that time. His fate was already assuming a definite shape; his sentence appeared to have been sealed in the course of the proceedings. Jill was his fiancée, and that can be embarrassing for one at times.

I only got to meet her again six months later. Enrique was no longer alive. I was starting to get a proper perspective on the whole story. I was being assailed by my headaches around then, excruciating, unrelenting headaches.

So I looked Estella up (or rather let's stay with Jill). She was married by then, to a certain Anibal Roque T., a highly reputable entrepreneur. I asked to have a chat with her in the morning. How scared she was, the lambkin! And how amenable once she was over the big relief! . . .

I am mulling over what could have drawn Enrique to Jill. Something irresistible, some kind of compulsion. I've said it before, and I'll say it again: I understand nothing about what makes the mind tick, my own least of all. I sensed one thing only, but that I was sure about, which is that everybody would have a price to pay in this case, everybody. I therefore had to enlighten her too that she would not get out of it scot-free. Maria was grieving; she had to pay in a different way. Jill was aware of that, don't think she wasn't, or why would she have agreed? Maybe out of fear primarily—I gave her reason enough, there's no question. But not solely out of fear—I'd be willing to swear to that whenever you wish. Jill was crafty: she tried to give our relationship the appearance of blackmail, and she could have come up with a pretext for it, as I say, but she never managed fully to convince me of this. As for herself, that's a good question. Did she perhaps wish to make amends in the way that I sought an accomplice in her? Did she pity me or despise me? I considered that was her business, but the case would not permit anyone to remain clean who had played any part in it, and Jill too must have learned that, I suppose, whatever she might have dreamed of when she hastily got married.

A sweet yet anguished relationship it was, inexcusable, I admit it. But in all likelihood that was precisely the attraction. Some crazy compulsion once drove me to the point of reading to her from Enrique's diary. That wasn't out of meanness, please believe me. What I mean is that I didn't read it to her in order to torment her, or so that I might—how the devil should I put this?—get a kick out of it. No way was there anything sexual in it. It was just that Enrique's shade was settling on me, and I felt it was too massive. I wanted it to settle over both of us. I had that right, whatever you may say, I had the right, since we owed each other. Enrique's shade settled on both of us. I wanted us to carry it together, to go around together beneath it, as if we were under a huge, monstrous umbrella, two lost souls in a storm . . .

It was a silly thing to do! She became upset, threw herself onto the bed, and screamed. She called us all murderers: me, Enrique, all men, life as a whole.

"Murderers!" she screamed.

"And you?" I ask. "What about you? You're a whore, an out-and-out tramp!" And believe it or not, I suddenly caught myself accusing her of treachery, and reproaching her for not having swung from the same rope as the accused, which is to say Enrique. I, who am supposed to be a flatfoot, after all.

Yet I understood Jill well: she was a woman, a woman first and foremost.

•  •  •

Anyway, there was this highway that led to the coast—
you know, to the bit where the peninsula pokes out into
the bay. Anyone traveling to the Blue Coast has to use
that road. That day Enrique and Jill drove to the Blue
Coast. They wanted to bathe. And Enrique was also
looking for someone at the beach.

He found who he was looking for—I'll be damned if
he didn't. That's where they all gathered, those shaggy-
haired weirdos. It was a shrewd choice: it's a big beach,
and they picked a secluded spot on it. They set down
their transistor radios, which put an end to our listening
devices. We photographed them, ten dozen rolls: they let
us do that, they were aware that they were known to us
anyway. We could have cracked down on them, sure we
could. But then what? They were pros; they weren't
doing anything. We wouldn't have dragged a word out
of them; what we would have been able to get from them
we knew anyway. It was all window dressing. They
didn't run many risks: it wasn't they who undertook the
actions. So what the hell were we supposed to do? We
kept them under observation until events caught up with
them. Then they all disappeared as if they had been
swallowed up by the earth. A confounded line of work
ours is; I wouldn't recommend it to anyone.

Among them was this C., whose name I won't spell

out. Enrique already mentioned him in his diary, if you recall. But Enrique wasn't the only one to document him, rest assured. I'll be a monkey's uncle if he didn't have a hand in the atrocity. But by the time we got wind that an atrocity was brewing, we could only snatch at thin air.

They would have nothing to do with Enrique. No way was it due to his money. There were wealthy kids in their ranks, more than one. Still, Enrique's money would surely have come in handy for them. No, the trouble was he was a greenhorn. They, as I said, were real pros. It would never have entered their minds to run risks. It was only Enrique, in his child's mind, who imagined he could just go up to them and enlist as if he were at a recruitment office.

He went over and found a happy bunch of students who amused him with their funny tales of university life. Each knew about a case, and the others would split their sides laughing.

Well, that's what happened. Enrique then trailed back to Jill. She looked stunning in her jazzy dress on the beach that day, and even more stunning out of it. Enrique, however, was furious.

"Forget them," Jill consoled him. "You aren't one of them."

"Why?" Enrique fumed. "Because my name is Salinas? Does that define a person?"

"You're bourgeois," Jill teased. She poked an index finger into the curly fuzz of hair on Enrique's chest and gently scratched with her nail. That is a detail I got from Enrique's diary. "You're bourgeois, bourgeois. My little bourgeois," she purred.

Enrique, however, was furious.

"Forget them," Jill said. "It's me you should concern yourself with now. Isn't it great here? Why don't you want to be happy?"

"Happy! Happy! . . ." Enrique fumed. But then, nice and slowly, he calmed down. From the scratching, I suppose. "Of course I want to be happy," he said. "I love you, don't I, God help me! But there are times when being happy—just happy, nothing else—is simply vile."

"Why?" Jill inquired, her eyes half closed. The sunlight was blindingly strong that day.

"Because," Enrique reasoned, "one can't be happy in a place where everybody is unhappy."

"Everybody?" Jill opened her eyes. "Look at me. I'm not." She smiled. One could well believe that she was not unhappy.

What could Enrique do? He kissed her. After that they walked out to the water. The sea was warm, there were not many people around, and they swam out a fair distance. In Jill's arms Enrique soon forgot about his frustration as well as his philosophy.

Only on the way home did it come to his mind again. On the highway.

Enrique's Alfa Romeo was speeding homeward with him at the wheel, Jill beside him. Their hair was fluttering, they raced along—until they came to a minimum speed sign. At that point Enrique took his foot off the gas and slowed to less than half the stipulated speed.

I need to say something about this highway. Some of you may not have been down that way, or else you don't recall it too well. Or maybe you never noticed anything special about it. That can happen: after all, that's what the minimum speed limit is for. Then again, some people only ever keep their eyes to the front. Lucky dogs: I always envied them.

In a nutshell, one of our establishments was situated out that way. Not exactly by the side of the road, but not far from it either. Those of you who have been there will know what I'm talking about. Our post was equipped with all the necessary paraphernalia: fences, electronics, watchtowers, and whatnot. Anyone who passed by and looked would have seen it—the outside, that is, not much more. We could hardly have shut down the highway as that would have forced the already-faltering commercial traffic into a detour around half the country. We could not force a bypass through, on account of the mountain chain: that sort of thing is pricey and might not even have been approved by parliament. You will have to ask their honors, the parliamentary representatives, whether they were aware of the situation and see what answers you get. Of course, they didn't have a clue about anything. The only option that was left, therefore, was to set a minimum speed limit. That way people would not be able to see very much, though undoubtedly something. The Colonel didn't mind that: a good citizen should be able to turn such a warning to his advantage. We set a fifty mph limit, but Enrique slowed down to twenty, according to the report that was issued on the traffic violation, and as was borne out by the appended photograph.

Jill was nervous—you bet she was. On top of which, Enrique wanted her to look in the direction of the establishment, but she didn't feel like doing that.

"What do want from me?"

"Why don't you want to look at it?" asked Enrique.

"Because it's none of my business," Jill fretted.

"So what is any of your business?" he pressed.

"You," she said.

"Well then," he plugged away, "that too is your business, because that is part of what I am."

"That's not true," she protested. "You're kidding yourself, Enrique. A normal person doesn't concern himself constantly with that sort of thing. To you it's nothing more than a drug. Whereas I, on the other hand, am sincere. Why can't we love each other, Enrique? I want to be happy. I want to bear your children. Nothing else is of interest to me."

"You're a clever girl, Jill. I envy you. You don't groan under the iron fist of dictatorship, you purr," so Enrique. At least according to the diary, and Jill later confirmed it. "Why don't you wish to take notice of it?"

"Because it doesn't interest me," she said. She was starting to get nettled.

"Jill," he said, "you're talking as if you hated the people who are being kept over there, behind the fence."

"That's right," she confirmed. "I hate them, because they're standing between us."

Right then a police car howled up alongside, overtook them, then cut across to block the way ahead. Enrique was obliged to stop.

I dare say you know how it goes. A screeching of brakes, doors bursting open, boots thudding on the concrete highway. A pair does the work, one covers with a semiautomatic handgun. "Step out of there! Make it snappy, or I'll drag you out! Upper body against the car, arms to the front, fingers spread!"

Something like that. A bit of jostling is unavoidable. Then the frisking. Women's dresses are particularly suspicious—they have room for all manner of things. A lovely female body, for example. Jill carried a bruise on her breast for a long time afterward.

Luckily, no camera was found either on them or in the car, I should note. Nor any other suspicious articles. Even so, the senior patrolman wanted to arrest them. And then he set eyes on Enrique's driver's license.

"Salinas," he reads. He casts an eye at the car. "The department store fellow?" he inquired.

He did not get an immediate answer.

"Right," he heard finally. Not from Enrique, but from Jill.

"I'm asking you, Jack!" The patrolman gave Enrique a tap on the leg with a boot tip.

"You heard," growled Enrique. The officer got ready to let fly, but his senior held him back.

"Didn't you see the speed sign?" he asked. It was not exactly keen cross-questioning, but then they don't always put the brightest men on highway patrol duty.

"Yes, I did," said Enrique.

"Then why didn't you keep to the limit?" the patrolman probed.

"I think one of the spark plugs is on the blink," Enrique ventured.

"On the blink, my ass," the senior patrolman opined. "You'd do better hitting your study books than bumming along the highway!"

"Then they should reopen the university," Enrique suggested. Now the senior patrolman was about to let fly, but he thought better of it. A Salinas was a Salinas, after all.

"Clear off," he ordered them. "I'll be making a report. I hope your father wrings your neck."

They continued their journey, side by side, Enrique at the wheel, Jill beside him. They were wordless, as if they did not know each other.

"Even so," Enrique broke the silence, without casting a glance at Jill, "it wouldn't hurt me to have at least an idea about what's going on."

"What would that be?" Jill shrugged. "Nothing." She fell silent. "Except I just hate you."

"I don't hate you, Jill," he said. "I'm just sorry that this is the way you feel."

"It makes no difference. The main thing is we don't wish to see each other ever again," she stated.

"True," he concurred.

They said no more. That was how they reached the city: wordlessly.

Enrique felt that at least now he knew what he wanted to know.

Something else happened that evening, something important, Enrique noted in his diary. Those few pages are like the record of a grilling—a genuine police interview in which he incriminated himself.

That was Enrique for you. He loved and hated, he was secretive and yet kept exhaustive records of his secrets.

I am opening Enrique's diary. Listen to this.

It's all been decided. Utterly unbelievable, and yet the most natural of all. It's as if, at the depths of my most hidden instincts, I had actually long suspected it. I must write it down: I can't go to bed now with this experience on my mind.

Let me try to sum up. That will be hard, so much has happened today, and now, late in the evening, all the complexions and events of this whole implausible day are spinning around at once in my head. Let's get on with it, then.

So I drove Jill home: I owed her that much. Then I came home myself. I parked the car in the garage, stepped into the elevator, and came up. As I entered the apartment, I caught sight of Mother and Father somewhere in the deceptive succession of interconnected rooms. They were a long way off, each seated in an armchair. Father was wreathed in fragrant clouds of smoke. He was stretching out his long, muscular legs, his black patent-leather shoes gleaming in the twilight. He had unbuttoned the jacket of his impeccable suit and loosened his fashionable necktie.

Mother was sitting with a straight back, hands resting in her lap.

It was as though they were just waiting for something.

When they spotted me, Mother immediately jumped up and rushed toward me. The usual stuff: "Where were you?" "At the beach." "You took a long time about it." "Because the weather was fine." One thing and another.

The old man did not stir, just kept on puffing on his cigarette. Finally, I said I needed a word with him. "Very well." He got to his feet and let me go first, gesturing toward his study with one hand, the other loosely gripping my shoulder. I sensed his aroma: a smell of tobacco, cologne, and Father. All at once I also sensed the hand resting on my shoulder. Strength emanated from it. Strength, superiority, and assurance. It was stupid, but I nearly burst into tears so that he might take me in his arms, as he had done when I was a child. Maybe on account of Jill.

No matter. Anyway, I briefly told him the about business on the highway, just the essentials. He didn't bat an eyelid.

"Did they find a camera on you?" he asked.

"No," I said. By sheer accident—though I don't say that to him. I had in fact intended to take some snapshots of Jill, but in my hurry I'd left the thing at home.

"They'll probably fine you," he dismissed the matter. "We'll pay it off. A good thing we can still afford it." He cracked a smile. He didn't seem too upset. "What were you looking for out there?"

"I was at the beach."

"On your own?"

"No."

"And you took it into your heads to have a kiss and cuddle there, of all places?" He smirked.

I became cross. I don't like it when the old man makes fun of my sexual desires. "We weren't kissing."

"Well what, then?"

"I wanted to show her something interesting out that way."

"I see." Father nodded, then got up and started to pace around the room. I was beginning to think he had forgotten me when all of a sudden I sensed him behind me. He placed a hand on my head.

"Enrique," I hear his voice, "how do you spend your days?"

I shrugged my shoulders. What on earth was I supposed to say?

"Son," he said, still in the same position, "Mother is worried about you." Silly things come to my mind. I'm on my way to school, and he says: "Take care, son, Mother is worried about you." Or I'm given my first car: "Be careful, son, Mother is worried about you." Only ever "Mother," never himself.

I didn't know what to say, or even how to indicate what was coming to mind.

He walked away and sat down behind his desk, facing me. He switched the lamp on. It was already evening. All kinds of dark, heavy shadows stretching out in all directions into the room beyond the yellowish cone of light from the reading lamp. A homely feeling.

"Son," he struck up again, "why aren't you being straight with me? We have time. I'm listening."

I let it all out then. Just as it came, disjointedly, angrily. Maybe that was the influence of Jill. I told him what I thought about it all. I told him I spent my days with nothing else but that occupying me, just that.

He heard me out very gravely, even though

most of what I said was probably drivel, as I was rather on edge. Still, I could see he was taking it seriously—as seriously as I was myself. He had never looked at me that way before. It was as if he wanted to see right through me. And he had to have seen, because I wanted him to see that I wasn't joking.

When I finished, he again got to his feet and swept his eyes round the room a few times, then sat back down.

"Is that just your opinion, Enrique," he asked, "or is it more than that?"

"What do you mean, Dad?"

"Are you still a free agent," he replied, "or are you already working . . . ," he hesitated, "for certain somebodies?" He spat it out in the end, just as stupidly as I did a few weeks ago to R.

"Not yet," I said.

"Not yet," he repeated. "In other words, you've tried?"

"Yes."

"And?"

"I've come up against certain obstacles."

He nodded. "Such as being called Salinas, for example."

"For example," I replied.

There was a glint in his eyes, which I took to be gloating. Again it nettled me.

"But it's a barrier that can be broken through, Dad," I continued. "With patience and determination it's possible to break through. I believe that, and I'll prove it, just wait and see!"

Solemnly he ran an inquiring look over my face, which had a hard expression on it, I could feel. It was a strange duel, and at the time its strangeness was all I perceived. Now, of course, I can see its sense as well.

"Listen to me, Enrique," he spoke again. "I have information from reliable sources that they are going to reopen the university before too long."

"Too bad," I commented. "We'll be under even closer scrutiny; they'll be able to step up surveillance."

"Undoubtedly." He nodded. "But you'll be able to continue your studies."

"I don't wish to continue them," I said. "There's no point."

"You mustn't forget about your future, Enrique."

"I'm living for the present, Dad."

"Ah!" He waved that aside. "The present is just temporary."

66

I boiled up. "I know," I burst out. "It only has to be accepted temporarily—temporarily, but every day afresh. And every day ever more. Temporarily. Until we have lived to the end of our temporary lives, and one fine day we temporarily die. Well, not for me, Dad! No and again no!"

"What do you want, Enrique?" he asked.

"Something definitive," I answered. "Something solid and permanent. Something that is me." And all of a sudden I came out with it: "I want to act. I want to change my way of life, Dad."

He seemed to wince, but why worry about that! I heard only my own voice as it came out at last with my innermost desire, so categorically that at a stroke I felt everything had become simple and clear. I had nothing more to say, I wanted to get up and leave the room. Then I heard him speaking:

"This is all just a figment of your imagination, Enrique. But a figment that at any moment can turn into a bloody reality." I don't know what sort of gesture I made, but he raised his hands and pinned me to the chair with his fingertips. "I heard you out," he carried on. "I expect you now to hear me out."

He was right, and I decided to do that. I would do whatever he might say. I would listen to him as calmly as possible, then answer his presumably dreary, predictable questions.

He duly began probing me, as if to test my patience and tenacity. As though he were trying to extract a confession. How was I to know that's what he was actually doing?

"Enrique," he began, "let's be serious. Maybe you will consider me cynical: I don't mind. But I'm your father, and my worries give me the right to speak. And anyway these are questions that you are going to have to face up to if, as you say, you wish to take action."

He paused. He pushed the cigarette box over to me. We lit up.

"You do realize, don't you," he kicked off, "that there isn't a single rational reason for someone who is called Salinas to be in the resistance?"

"It's not clear to me where you draw the bounds of rationality, Dad," I riposted.

"At realities, Enrique. Only ever at realities."

"Money, in other words."

"Yes, money too, among other things. But not just money." He pondered, as if he were searching for the most apposite word. "Let's just say at the means of earning a livelihood," he eventually declared. "We have the means to live. Or to put it another way, we have the means of surviving: that is what I wanted to say in essence."

"Yes," I said, "there's no doubt about that!"

"You do realize, don't you," he went on, "that we not only have the means to live but, more than that, to live in security? . . . Wait!" He raised a hand before I had a chance to respond. "Do you know what uncertainty is?"

I had to think about that. "Yes, I do," I eventually said.

"How do you know?"

"I learned today, on the highway. When that cop brushed me with his boot tip. If I weren't called Salinas, they would have beaten me to a pulp, I think."

"Indeed." He nodded. "I wasn't in a position to refer to that. I'm glad you got wise to that of your own accord, Enrique. You do realize then, don't you, that if you risk your neck, you'll be doing so for others, not yourself?"

His question again gave me pause. "Within the narrow bounds that you've set, I have to concede that that is so," I said at length.

"The bounds are always narrow." He leaned toward me from behind the desk. "If a person resolves to fight, he ought to know what he is fighting for. Otherwise it makes no sense. A person usually fights against a power in order to gain power himself. Or else because the power in question is threatening his life. You have to acknowledge, though, that in our case neither of these holds true."

"Sure, I acknowledge it," I said. The game was beginning to intrigue me. A ghastly game it was, in point of fact; I felt a strange chill around my heart. I can't define it more precisely than that. I felt that he was right, that every word he was saying was right, and yet my entire innermost being protested against that truth. I feared that by the end of the conversation I would have no choice but to loathe my father, whom I loved. And I was afraid of that fear, a hundred times more afraid of that than I was of the truth of his arguments.

"You do realize, don't you," I heard his voice continue, "you do realize that every faction with a sense of purpose needs its unsuspecting tools. Who are tools even though they are called heroes, and even if statues are erected to a few of them— only ever a very few—in public places."

"I know," I mumbled hoarsely.

"You do realize, Enrique, you do realize, don't you, what you're putting at risk?"

Again I had to think about it.

"My life," I eventually said.

"Your life!" he exclaimed. "You say that as if you were a child throwing aside a rag doll that you're fed up with! Enrique, wake up to the fact that you're living among mere concepts and thinking in terms of empty words. You're putting your life at risk, you say, but you don't have a clue what you're talking about. Try to grasp the fact that your life is you yourself, as you are sitting here, with your very real past, a possible future, and everything that you mean to your mother. Look at this evening, look down at the street, look around you in the world, and imagine it all being here no more. Grab your body, pinch your flesh, and imagine all that being no more. Can you imagine it? Do you have any idea what it means: to live? How could you know? You're still young for that, and healthy . . . You've never been at death's door and come back from there to rediscover life with wonderstruck joy . . . But do you at least realize that you were lied to at school? Do you realize that there is no afterlife, nor any resurrection? Do you realize that just this one life is given to us, and if we lose it, we also lose ourselves? Do you realize . . ."

I listened, flabbergasted. His words were

spellbinding; I had never seen my father like this. I would never have thought him to be a coward. How was I to guess the purpose of his probing?

"I know," I said, striving to hold myself in check, though something was quivering inside me.

"Well, if you know," Father asked, "what more do you want? What's the point of fighting if you have no reason to fight? Why risk your life, if it's not in danger?" He got up from his place and came around to me. He leaned over me, grasping my shoulders with both hands. They were strong, very strong. "Why?" he entreated. "Tell me why. I want to know. Tell me!"

So I told him. I shook his hands off my shoulders and spilled it all out. Jill was still dancing in my nerves and lurking in my words. I told him that my life was not in danger, it was just that I could not be reconciled to it. "I would rather not have it," I said, "than live it like this." I talked about my itch to throw up, my abomination of everyday life. How I hated everything around me, everything. I hated their policemen, their newspapers, their news. I hated going into an office, a shop, even a café. I hated the furtive glances around me, the people who had been despised yesterday but were celebrated today.

I hated the sufferance, the self-interest, the hide-and-seek, the perpetual one-upmanship, the privileges and the lying doggo . . . Also the patrolman on the highway, who didn't have the guts to kick me, simply because my name is Salinas: I hated him more for that than for touching me with his boot. I hated the blindness, the bogus hope, the algal life, the stigmatized who, when they get a day's break from the lashes of the whip, immediately start to sigh about how good life is . . . And I hated myself too, myself above all, merely for being here and doing nothing. I was well aware that I too was stigmatized, for the time being at any rate, and the longer I did nothing, the more I would be so. Jill appeared before my eyes again, the nauseatingly seductive life that she offered me.

"And," I shouted, "in order to do more than just hate but bare my teeth as well, it's enough for me to think of myself dutifully taking my exams, starting a family and siring children, paying my taxes and tending flowers in my garden . . . In short, over time becoming a happy and well-balanced jailbird!"

I stopped talking and looked up into Father's smoldering eyes. Overcome by an odd feeling, I faltered. It was as though those mute eyes were looking right through me, as though they knew something that I didn't. Again I sensed his strength, and felt that I was a child.

I was disconcerted. "You can't understand," I said.

"Why do you suppose that?" he asked deliberately and gravely.

"Because . . . because . . ." I tried but couldn't find the right word. As if he had me in his power merely because his gravity, his strength, and his gaze towered over me.

"Do you think I'm a coward? A cynic? Stupid?" he asked.

"No, of course not. None of those things," I said. And all at once I found my own voice again. "It's just that you can't step over your own shadow."

"You think I'm middle class, a bourgeois. A property owner and stock market speculator. Right?"

I don't know if I did think that; I don't know if I could think that. When it comes down to it, that is what I am as well. I am privileged because he's my father. All the same, I said:

"Yes. And I can't come to terms with your patience."

"Why?" he asked.

I thought I was going to fall off the chair. He was as inexorable as an examining magistrate. Was I to start all over from the beginning?

"Because," I exclaimed, "I no longer have patience for even half an hour!" I jumped to my feet. "Don't you understand that I can't bear to go on living like this? I'm sick of doing nothing, of my situation, of mediocrity!" A good word that; I was pleased with it. "Yes, that's it: sick of mediocrity," I repeated. "Mediocrity is a sickness. Yes, Dad," I added. "Mediocrity is downright pathological!"

And I rushed off toward the study door. I felt that I had said all I had to say and that I should not allow myself to listen to any more of his arguments. And I felt that I had to escape from the force of his gravity and his gaze in order to be alone and truly able to stand up to him at last . . .

My hand was on the door handle when his voice arrested me.

"Stop, Enrique! Come back! Take your seat!" he commanded. And I obeyed him, as if . . . yes, as if I were just waiting for something more, I don't know what, but something more plausible—some deliverance from this nightmare.

I should note—though I don't know why I

consider it to be of any importance—that Dad was not sitting but standing behind his desk, leaning with his hands on the desktop. Not on the palms of his hands, to be precise, but on his ten splayed-out fingers, inclined slightly forward.

"I heard you out," he said. "You, however, have not heard me out." He paused. "I'll make you a proposal," he eventually continued. "Consider it. My proposal is that we work together, Enrique. Take part in the work of the sort of men to whom I belong."

I don't remember what he said. I mumbled something. All that I noted exactly was his response:

"Yes, Enrique, of course. Only I didn't know how seriously I could take you. But on the basis of what has been said, I conclude that I can count on you."

Thereupon he produced a bottle and two glasses from his cocktail cabinet. We clinked glasses. Then we chatted, very seriously for a long time before going across into the dining room. Mother was already seated in her place, dishing out the supper. I ate well, with a hearty appetite.

I am closing Enrique's diary: I have no further need of it. The rest was our business—Diaz's, Rodriguez's, and mine, the new boy's. Oh, and a matter of the logic that led us to Enrique and Enrique to us.

That logic was not without its flaws. Who said it was? It was initially more just an idea; only later did it become logical. At that point, for instance, we were not aware of Enrique's diary. How would we have been? It came into our hands only in the course of the house search. And even then none of us read right through it: we didn't need to, and above all, we didn't have the time. Things were getting distinctly uncomfortable for us around that time, with incidents coming thick and fast. The Colonel was nervous. We had got wind of an impending atrocity. We had to prevent it, or at least try, with every means at our disposal: Homeland and Colonel demanded that of us. The shaggy-haired weirdos all went into hiding. We circulated their details nationally but with about as much success as if we had been searching, let's say, for half a dozen irregularly yellow-striped Colorado beetles in a twenty-five-thousand-acre field of potatoes.

We had to go with what was on hand, in other words. And Enrique happened to be on hand. We identified him in a photo among the people who were not on hand. How had he found his way into the photograph? Was he one of them? If he was, why hadn't he gone into hiding as well? Might he have been left as bait? Or did he have an assignment out in the open? In which case, how could they have let him find his way into a photograph? Or did he have nothing to do with them and appeared in it only by chance?

Questions and yet more questions. We had no time to fiddle around with questions. A huge mechanized apparatus, with records, informers, and all those flatfeet, was looking for something to do: we were set up for organizing, for taking action, not for solving crossword puzzles. We did the broad-brush stuff, not the finicky detailed work. Enrique's name came up in a search of the records: there was a squeal on him from Ramón. Then that offense on the highway. And now the photo. All of these bits had been there previously, properly filed: we hadn't taken a look at him. Now, though, we wheeled him in because we needed him, and that altered the complexion of things. Everything is a matter of logic. Events per se mean nothing. Life itself can be regarded as an accident. The function of the police, however, is to bring logic to bear on Creation, as I heard Diaz say many a time. A wise man, Diaz was. I personally did not have much liking for him; he caused me a lot of headaches. But never in my life did I see a flatfoot to beat Diaz. No getting round it. He was born for the work—it was his vocation. Above all, he knew what he wanted, and in our line of work that's a big deal.

In short, as I say, we were groping around in the dark, metaphorically as well as literally. We sat in a darkroom and had photographs developed and then enlarged. The individuals who were visible in the enlarged shots were then identified, one by one. As I said, we had shot ten dozen rolls of film of them at the Blue Coast and wherever else.

Well anyway, in one of the Blue Coast photos we spotted a new face. He is standing there in the group of wanted individuals. They are laughing, while he seems rather sullen. Ramón immediately identified him as Enrique Salinas. We could have identified him without Ramón's help, but what's an informer for if not to make himself useful?

From that moment on Enrique Salinas did not take a step without our knowing about it.

One week later we received a film reel from our people. An interesting movie it was, a worthy reward for our troubles.

Enrique can be seen in it. He enters a café. He is carrying a briefcase. He takes a seat at a table.

Cut.

A chap arrives at the café. A nondescript character, middle-aged, medium height, no distinguishing marks. He is carrying a briefcase. After a brief hesitation, he recognizes Enrique and sits down at his table. They are discussing something, hastily spreading out documents from their briefcases.

Enrique also produces an envelope from his case.

As the papers are being tidied up, that envelope is slipped among the stranger's documents.

The chap pockets the envelope.

They finish their discussion and put the files away. They pay and leave, separately.



So much for the film. We found out that the chap was called Manuel Figueras, a sales clerk who had worked for a few years for the Salinas stores. A married man, he had two children. He had no lover, and his name didn't turn up in our records. The Salinas company's personnel department, where we had one of our people (why would we not have one there, of all places?), could tell us nothing about him of any interest.

Figueras hurried from the café straight back to his office. He went by bus, having left his beat-up Volkswagen in the big parking lot in front of the Salinas office building. He only popped up again once work was over: he got into his Volkswagen and drove straight home.

Over the ensuing days Figueras traveled only between his office and home. We tailed him on his journeys, but he didn't have a telephone for us to tap. His partner was a housewife; she had no lover. Her time was entirely taken up with housework; we noticed nothing suspicious about her shopping trips. Their ten-year-old boy attended school; the four-year-old girl we discounted. On Saturday evening Figueras went with his wife to see a movie. On Sunday afternoon he took his son to watch a soccer match. Never even once did he make contact with strangers. What had he done with the envelope? Was it still on him, perhaps? Or had he passed it on? Might it have been addressed directly to him? We had no way of knowing.

Ten days later Enrique Salinas's Alfa Romeo headed out of the city and turned onto the southwestern trunk road. He stopped in B., the region's fashionable seaside resort. He checked into a room in a busy hotel, using his own name. That evening he went down to the bar. It was hot, and he was lightly dressed in slacks and a colorful, high-necked silk shirt. He was presumed not to have a briefcase—our men came across it when they searched his room during his absence. Among other things they found inside was an envelope containing a folded sheet of white paper. It bore the number "3" in the top left-hand corner and in the middle were six typewritten letters in the sequence ENAUSE. The envelope was resealed with an appropriate technique, and all traces of our search were removed.

The next morning Figueras's beat-up Volkswagen headed out of the city and turned onto the southwestern trunk road. He stopped in B. and parked his car in front of Enrique Salinas's hotel. He went into the hotel's bar and ordered himself a drink.

At precisely eleven o'clock, Enrique Salinas came down from his room and looked into the bar. Undoubtedly, he noticed Figueras. He left without having taken a seat.

Figueras soon paid and returned to the parking lot. There he found Enrique Salinas, who was fussing with something under the hood of his Alfa Romeo. They greeted each other like old acquaintances. Figueras got into his own car, then for a minute Enrique Salinas—in the midst of speaking to him—climbed in beside him. On this occasion our man, from his adverse position, saw nothing, but he presumed that at this moment Enrique must have passed the envelope on to Figueras.

Afterward, Figueras promptly started up the engine and, on getting back to the city, did not stop until he reached the Salinas office building. He entered the building right away and did not leave it again that day until work was over. Then he again hurried directly to his parking space. He was extremely surprised to find, in the spot where he had presumed his Volkswagen would be, a black limousine. Twenty minutes later he found himself at Corps headquarters. We set about interrogating him without further ado.

I am unhappy talking about this, especially going into

details. All the newspapers have printed enough bull-shit about this sort of thing nowadays; everybody now knows how that sort of thing goes: roughly the way they can see in their idiotic movies, just a bit more to the point. And well, with the difference that everything is for real.

It's nasty work, I can tell you, but it's part of the job. We take away the offender's mind, shred his nerves, par-alyze his brain, rifle through every pocket and even his innards. We slam him into a chair, draw the curtains, light a lamp—in short, we go by the book. We didn't make any effort to surprise the offender with some origi-nal twist. Everything happened in the way those ham-handed films would have prepared him for; everything happened the way he would expect; and precisely that was always the surprise—check it out if you don't believe me. We gather around, with Diaz facing him, Rodriguez to the side, me behind.

Then out comes the line. And a flood of questions, simply deluging him.

"Right, pig," one of us will kick off. "Playtime's over. You've been rumbled."

"We know everything," another interjects. "You'll only be hurting yourself if you try to deny anything."

"Young Enrique's already spilled the beans. You'd be well advised to do the same."

"It's in your interest. It's all the same to us."

"It's difficult, we know, but if you're a good boy, you can be let off. Bear that in mind."

"What's the point of getting your nuts crushed if your accomplice has already spilled the beans?"

"So be a good boy, open your mouth. Or are we going to have to open it for you?!"

"Who's your go-between?"

"Where's the envelope?" (A body search had not revealed it on him.)

"Where's your weapons dump?"

"When are you planning for the atrocity to happen?"

"Which group do you belong to? Spit it out!"

"You've no choice anyway. Let yourself go, be sensible!"

"Be sensible, then you'll soon be rid of us."

"Your accomplices have hung you out to dry. Do you want to carry the can alone? In their place?"

"Not talking, then?"

This was all bluff, as you can see, to prepare the ground. We stun him with a deluge of questions. He has to feel that he is utterly alone, whereas there are a lot of us; that we are able to do with him what we want; and that we know everything, much more than he could suspect. But that we've got it all wrong, and he's the only one who can set us straight, if he wishes to improve his circumstances. It's a stale old number, but it usually works. If you know of a better one, say so.

We then slowly get around to what is actually of interest to us. What we wanted to know from Figueras, for instance, was the story behind the envelope. We found out as well, though don't push me on how. Figueras couldn't cut it; Rodriguez wasted his time working on him, because what he had to say he spat out right away, and after that we were unable to drag anything further out of him.

In such cases Diaz would fill out a request form and call for the duty guard. Everybody had their place with us, and if the Homeland's security was under threat, we weren't accountable to anyone.

The three of us were left to ourselves. It was a wretched moment, that goes without saying. Just look at what we had extracted from Figueras. Federigo Salinas had sent him out to collect the envelopes. Beforehand he had been called into the boss's office, and was offered extra pay for his work. "It's a matter of confidential stock market tip-offs," Figueras claims Salinas told him. It was a delicate matter of the sort that comes up not infrequently in business life; that was why he was asking him, Figueras, and not one of his managers, who might be recognized by the network's agents. And that was why he asked Figueras to stick to certain precautionary measures. Figueras did not get nosy: he was a small fry who was glad for the confidence that was being shown in him and for the unexpected income. According to his statement, he didn't know that Enrique Salinas was the boss's son. We could believe him: never once during the whole time that we had him under observation did Enrique Salinas turn up at the Salinas office building. The first time Figueras met him was on the basis of a verbal description; on subsequent occasions he recognized the face. Figueras would then hand on the envelopes to Federigo Salinas.

Well, you make head or tail of that. We tried. We put it together, took it apart, then pieced it together again and worked our way through it afresh.

Question: From whom did Enrique get the envelopes? Figueras didn't know, and frankly neither did we, even though we were watching every step Enrique made.

Furthermore: Why didn't Enrique simply hand the envelopes over to his father himself? We had only one possible explanation: Enrique was not supposed to see his father's role—or maybe even his involvement—in the network, and he was not supposed to know that the envelopes were going to him. If that were so, then perhaps Federigo Salinas was pulling all the strings in the background and we had stumbled on one of the Uprising's top men, if not its clandestine leader. Rodriguez, for one, was quite sure of this possibility. The work excited him; his leopard eyes smoldered and kept coming to rest on the statuette that adorned his desk.

You can't do a good job without method, however. We had to crack the first question above all.

The answer to that, though, could only come from Enrique.

"Enrique Salinas," said Diaz. "You, Martens, will make the arrest. But not at his home. Grab him anywhere else. And don't make a fuss about it."

Well, I didn't. I snatched him on the street with my men the next day, around eleven o'clock, when he was on his way back from B. We waited for him to park his car in the garage, then take the elevator to his apartment. Obviously, he would have let his mother know he was back; a bit later he popped down to the street for something. We simply bundled him into the limousine in the traffic. We have specialists for that. By the time he realized what was happening, he was sitting between us, one wrist handcuffed to me, the other to my man.

"What do you want? Who are you?" he asked.

We kept quiet, as is our practice.

"The police? The Corps?" he had another go, then he shut up. He held his peace when we got out and led him across the Headquarters' forbidding inner courtyards, and he held his peace as we took him down the long series of corridors where detainees were pressing hands and foreheads to the walls, with alert guards at their backs. That was our practice. That too was part of preparing the ground.

He held his peace above all when Diaz set about questioning him. Diaz was gentle with him, and I don't mean with that diabolical meekness of his—he was unusually gentle. On this occasion he personally took over the interrogation, and he did not want there to be any fanfare.

"We have a few questions for you. We are proceeding on the assumption that you personally are innocent. If you give us satisfactory answers, you can go home afterward," said Diaz.

Enrique, however, did not answer a single question. I knew that he must be quaking inwardly, he had to be, but his expression remained set, like a clenched fist. And he held his peace, resolutely held his peace.

"Listen," Diaz asked him, "you do appreciate where you are, don't you? We don't make a habit of pussyfooting around. We can conduct this conversation in a very different way."

Enrique, however, held his peace. He stubbornly held his peace, with stupid determination. Rodriguez and I just sat there, condemned to inactivity. At that time I didn't understand what Diaz was up to, didn't understand him at all. Could he have miscalculated, just this once? Had he perhaps applied the wrong technique?

Now I am less inclined to think so. Now I can see more clearly what sort of stakes Diaz was playing for. But well, I was still a new boy, as I have said, and I didn't yet have a view of what went on behind the scenes; I was taken in by what happened before my eyes. Now I am not so sure that Diaz really wanted Enrique to talk. If he had really wanted it so much, then he would not have proceeded on the assumption that Enrique was innocent. Or at least he would not have said that to his face. He was too good a detective to do that, was Diaz, far too good.

"Well?" he inquired mildly, facing Enrique, one buttock perched on the desk, as per habit.

Enrique, however, held his peace. After waiting a bit, Diaz leaned forward. In fact he was mild-mannered even now, mild-mannered and patient. Only I could truly see how much he was. Enrique most likely could have had no conception at all; most likely all he sensed was that his nose had started to bleed.

"Well?" Diaz asked.

And then a strange thing happened. As Diaz was leaning toward him, Enrique spat a huge gob of phlegm in his face. A strange thing, that was. And not just strange: dilettante, I would have to say. Yes, that's what I would have to say. No one spits in Diaz's face. Not that Diaz doesn't give people a thousand reasons to do so; it's just that it's both futile and risky, and one doesn't run risks for something futile. It takes a profound bitterness, at the very least, or a profound ignorance. Whichever the case, no one who has any interest in living, real living, spits in Diaz's face. During my career nothing like that ever happened again.

To be brief, an uneasy foreboding for Enrique sprang up that was subsequently never to leave me. He alarmed me because all of a sudden I sensed that he was innocent. He was innocent, and his innocence was intransigent, like a virginity that has been violated. It was a lousy feeling, made all the lousier by the fact that I had no one to speak to about it.

I noticed that it was also bothering Diaz. Not that Diaz said anything; he slipped off the desk and absent-mindedly mopped his face. He then strode up and down the room a few times, hands clasped behind his back. As I have said, that was his habit when he was thinking. He harrumphed a few times. He finally came to a standstill behind Enrique and placed a hand on his head.

"What a big meathead you are, dear boy," he said. "A very big meathead." At this point, Rodriguez, whose impatient fingers had been fiddling with his model the whole time, finally got up from his place.

Minutes passed, long minutes, and then he brought him back from next door. I was looking at Diaz. It's interesting that this time Diaz did not perch on the desk.

Diaz was looking sideways at something, I don't know what.

"Well?" he asked.

But Enrique gave no answer. He couldn't. He was asleep, or whatever.

Then Diaz looked at him.

"Meathead!" he said to Rodriguez. "What in God's name did you do to the kid!"


So that was how it stood. We could not expect a statement from Enrique anytime soon—certainly not without hospital treatment. Diaz had made no allowance for this possibility. Or so it seemed. Now I would not care to take an oath on that. At the time, though, being a new boy, I was still taken in by what happened before my eyes, as I said. Diaz knew his men, and he knew very well what he wanted. It would have been hard for anyone to surprise him, although that didn't occur to me at the time.

He did not reproach Rodriguez for what he had done. Diaz wasn't one for idle words. He was a man of hard facts, and what had happened was now a fact. He had to keep moving ahead, always ahead. There was truth in Diaz's logic, yes: our line of work is like that. Once you've started, the only way back is to go forward.

"Salinas ought to be brought in," said Rodriguez.

"Right." Diaz nodded.

"Should I bring him in?" Rodriguez offered.

"No," Diaz gestured.

As the two of them were speaking, they took no notice of me. I just sat and listened. My head was aching, aching horribly. Maybe it showed.

"He'll skip town," Rodriguez worried.

"Where to?" Diaz riposted.

"How should I know! That sort always has somewhere!" Rodriguez fretted. "Give me the slip at the very last moment, the rotten bourgeois."

"We're not fighting capitalism as such," Diaz reminded him.

"It's all the same to me." Rodriguez's eyes were smoldering. "Bourgeois, Jew, savior of the world—there's nothing to choose between them. Upheaval is all they want."

"And you?" Diaz inquired. "What do you want, Rodriguez, my son?"

"Order. But my order," said Rodriguez. "Should I go?"

"No. We'll wait." Diaz strode up and down the room a few times, hands clasped behind his back. "It's noon now. You boys go home and get some shut-eye. Be back here by seven this evening. Prepare for what may be an all-night session. We may well have plenty of work."

He said no more. I'll be a Dutchman if I could even guess what he had in mind. But that was Diaz for you. For my own part, I was always glad for the unexpected gift of a few hours off duty. The job takes its toll, so we richly deserve the occasional bit of R&R.

There was a time when I would have preferred to spend those few hours with Diaz. I would have been curious about how he wove the web of his logic and about how he won over the Colonel, for example.

I now see the answer as simple: he just set the facts before him. And the Colonel had no option but to move ahead: for him too the only way back was to go forward. Everyone had their part to play in this game, as I said, Enrique just as much as the Colonel. And Diaz as well, who imagined that it was he who assigned the roles. Diaz was also built into the logic; the Colonel must have known him in just the same way as Diaz knew Rodriguez, for instance. No, there was no longer room for anyone here outside the logic.

Anyway, to be brief, we reassembled at seven o'clock. By then Diaz had the authorization in his hands. It had to be: this was work for which authorization was needed. Not a broad authorization, that would not have been sufficient, but a special authorization. And don't go thinking that I had any idea of this at the time. Diaz said not a word to us; he didn't need to. We followed him blindly down the path of the logic: he was our commander, we couldn't object.

We sat and waited, blew smoke rings. It was warm, and my headache had barely eased up. The telephone rang at nine o'clock that evening.

"Major Diaz," Diaz announced.

Shortly afterward, he said:

"I shall consider it a special honor to be of service to you, General." He said it in a tone of voice that was like he had oiled his tonsils beforehand.

Barely an hour later the commander of the guard reported. He had been given his instructions; everyone in Headquarters that day knew what they had to do. "A man identifying himself as Federigo Salinas, proprietor of the Salinas department store, is requesting an urgent hearing from the duty officer."

"Bring him up," Diaz declared elegantly into the handset. He then crossed his legs as if awaiting a round of applause. He would have deserved one, make no mistake. Only now could we see just how much a detective Diaz was.

Ten minutes later we were welcoming Federigo Salinas into our office. He arrived in a dark suit; he was distinguished, cool, and formal. Diaz bowed like a retired dancing master. There were times when Diaz could be smooth, confoundedly smooth.

"Permit me," he says, "to introduce my colleagues, Mr. Rodriguez and Mr. Martens."

Salinas barely glanced at us but nodded like a king from his throne. He was a real gentleman, was Salinas—he had an exquisite feel for that.

"Delighted," he says, though as far as that goes, he has no reason to be. "In point of fact I need to speak to the Colonel."

"The Colonel," cooed Diaz, "is preparing for a speech in parliament tomorrow."

"Everyone is using that excuse. I've been unable to reach him by telephone all evening," Salinas seethed. "Even though I asked intermediaries like Vargas, the banker, and General Mendoza to relay my request."

"I was speaking with the General just now," fawned Diaz. "Do take a seat, Mr. Salinas. We are at your disposal; you may trust in our discretion. Cigar?"

That's how it began. As stylish as one could wish, as you can see. Diaz didn't hurry Salinas along, just stalled him. Something was giving Salinas grief, that was evident, but Diaz waited tactfully, like a father-confessor.

In the end it was Salinas who ran out of patience first.

"In point of fact"—he nibbled at the hook—"it's about my son."

There was silence. Maybe he was awaiting a word of encouragement from Diaz. Diaz, however, stayed quiet, his bland expression showing only mild interest and an artless desire to be helpful.

"My son," says Salinas. "Well . . . at some point during the day my son vanished."

"Fancy that," Diaz registered surprise. "Vanished, you say?"

"Vanished," Salinas repeated.

"I'm afraid that's not the sort of case in which we have any competence," Diaz agonized. "Maybe you should make inquiries with the police or, if you're really worried, the ambulance service."

"They have no knowledge of him."

"I would point out"—Diaz cracked a smile—"that it's not unknown for young men to vanish unexpectedly for an evening or a night. There's no reason to think the worst right away when it happens."

"I don't doubt it," Salinas comes back. "In this case, though, allow me to proceed by my hunches, because at some point yesterday one of my clerks also vanished without a trace."

The conversation was starting to get interesting, distinctly interesting. And as though a chill had grown between the two of them, Salinas no longer had the old expression on his face.

"I still don't understand," says Diaz, "how we can be of assistance to you."

"You didn't bring him in?" Salinas asks, not even raising his voice. But I supposed that Salinas could give dirty looks, just as dirty as Diaz did on occasion.

"The only people we bring in," responds Diaz, "are individuals about whom we have reasonable grounds to be suspicious."

"I have to tell you in all frankness," Salinas says at this juncture, "that certain circumstances . . . quite innocent circumstances, I can assure you . . . might possibly have cast my son in a suspicious-looking light."

"So, according to your assumption, did he actually do anything?" Diaz asks.

"He's here?" says Salinas in response.

"According to your assumption, did he actually do anything on account of which he might be here?" Diaz reiterates.

"You've arrested him?" Salinas asks again.

Diaz was now looking at him far from pleasantly. "Mr. Salinas, you're posing very odd questions. And you're posing your odd questions in an odd way."

"Is he here, or isn't he?" Salinas leaped up. For a moment I thought he was going to grab Diaz by the lapels.

"Sit back down. We can't discuss anything like this.

It seems you are forgetting where you are, Mr. Salinas." Diaz's voice by now was unpleasant, distinctly unpleasant.

"I'm well aware of where I am. I came on my own steam. Are you trying to threaten me?" Salinas asks.

"No, just to remind you of the house rules," says Diaz.

"And what's that supposed to mean?!"

"Just that it's we who ask the questions here. We ask the questions, and you give the answers, Mr. Salinas."

At that point Diaz stands up and switches on the lamp. He makes his way ponderously around the desk and parks one buttock on it. Right in front of Salinas.

Rodriguez gets up and steps over to Salinas's side.

I move behind his back.

"What do you people want?" Salinas is startled.

"Nothing in particular, Mr. Salinas," Diaz replies. "We just have a few questions for you."

And so it begins—much as I have already described earlier.


Salinas proved a tough customer; he really tested our patience to the limit. He cracked only after we brought his son up—literally brought him, as he was unable to walk.

"Well?" asked Diaz.

"Not in front of my son," Salinas said dully after a while, his face buried in his hands.

"No way," said Diaz. "Otherwise we'll smash your bones. We'll leave the choice up to you."

Salinas soon thought better of his position.

Don't ask me to recall precisely who said what, or in which sequence. I don't recall even what I myself said. There was confusion, and my head ached. From time to time, when a burst of energy seized me, I would lean forward and ask something:

"From whom did Enrique get the envelopes?"

"From me."

"To whom did Figueras give the envelopes?"

"To me."

"Are you trying to tell me that you sent letters to yourself by way of Enrique and Figueras?!"

"Yes, that's how it was."

"Do you take us for fools?"

"I can't tell you anything else. That's what I did."

"And why did you do it?"

"To head off trouble, so my son would not take a fateful step of some kind."

"What kind of fateful step?"

"I was afraid that he was going to be recruited into some kind of student movement."

"So you recruited him instead, into your own secret network, huh?!"

"I have no secret network. No secret organization of any kind. I dreamed the whole thing up."

"What possible reason could you have had to do that?"

"I've already told you: to protect my son."

"And why did you need the letters to do that?"

"To indulge his flights of fancy and satisfy his craving for action. He wouldn't listen to sober arguments. I had to create the appearance that he was engaged in secret work."

"And he wasn't?"

"No. He's innocent. He is, and so is Figueras, and so am I. I can prove it."

"As yet, that's still a bit far away. What's the meaning of ENAUSE?"

"It's an anagram of the word *unease*. I put the word in each envelope. I've used three envelopes—"

"Two!"

"In that case you don't know about the first one. You were late in putting my son under surveillance. There are still two envelopes—"

"Where?"

"With Quintieros, the public notary. I deposited them with him."

"Why?"

"To cover my tracks and, should it be necessary, to be in a position to prove my son's innocence."

"You were a little late with that."

"I acted in his interest. He was rushing headlong into disaster. I was guided by my unease; I did it all for him. You have taken unfair advantage of his gullibility. Murderers! Bastards!"

A pause ensued, after which we returned to the envelopes.

"I placed an identical piece of paper in each envelope. I numbered them serially, and on each of them I printed ENAUSE. I printed all of them on my own typewriter so the lettering would be identifiable. You've overstepped your authority, and you'll all be answerable for that! The envelopes that are with Quintieros . . ."

And so it went on. Should I say I was surprised by what we learned from Salinas? That evening nothing surprised me any longer. Diaz, though, sprang to his feet as if he had been stung by a wasp. Now Diaz was generally a placid man. I had never seen him as nervous as he was then.

He leaned forward into Salinas's face:

"Do you take us for idiots?! Just who do you think we are? Ass-scratching lawyers who are going to tip their hats to your public notary? Do you suppose we haven't heard about double-bluffing? Do you suppose we are incapable of imagining that you are using one set of correspondence to conceal the other? Do you suppose we don't know how many ways there are to decipher a code? . . . Don't imagine you're going to break free from our clutches! Not until we have laid bare the whole truth!"

At which point it all started afresh, from the beginning.

Don't expect to learn what else happened that evening. It was no longer an interrogation but a poker game. I was still a new boy, as I have said; only then had I begun to see where I was and what I had taken on. I knew, of course, that a different yardstick applied in the Corps— but I believed there was at least a yardstick. Well, there wasn't: don't expect me to tell you what happened that evening.

We hauled in the public notary. We hauled him in because he had failed in his duty as a citizen to report a suspicious act; we hauled him in because that was what Diaz wanted. We surprised him at the dinner table, just as he was celebrating something or other. He was a self-assured fellow, the public notary; he protested and demanded a lawyer.

Later on, though, he just sat between us in his ripped shirt, his pomaded cheeks sunken, his fleshy lower lip drooping limply.

"I don't understand you, gentlemen," he mumbled. "I don't understand. What do you want from me? After all, the state places its trust in me!"

"That's as may be." Diaz nodded, almost like an elementary schoolteacher. "Only we don't place our trust in the state."

The notary just goggled at him with his tiny watery eyes. "I don't understand. I don't understand. In what do you place your trust then?"

"In destiny. Right now, though, we have taken on the role of destiny: so in ourselves." Diaz, one buttock on the desk, smiled his inimitable smile.

For me this was just like a message that Diaz had sent via the notary. I finally grasped his logic, or at least I believe I grasped it. I grasped that we had now cast away everything that bound us to the laws of man; I grasped that we could no longer place our trust in anyone except ourselves. Oh, and in destiny, in that insatiable, greedy, and eternally hungry mechanism. Were we still spinning it, or was it spinning us? Now it all amounts to the same thing. You think you are being very clever in riding events out, as I say, and then you find that all you want to know is where the hell they are galloping off to with you.

. . .

The interrogations went on for a while longer. We summoned witnesses, took statements, followed procedure. In the course of that procedure we drew the net of logic ever tighter. The Salinas file grew thicker. Then we set it aside. At the time, with unfavorable portents multiplying, we had a lot to do.

The tape-recorder spools spun on, though, automatically, inexorably, constantly in their slots. Recording their words, the sounds of their prison life that were no longer of any interest to anyone.

I listened to them many times, however. I'm sorry not to have them with me; I could make good use of them here, as all I have is Enrique's diary.

Still, they live on in my memory, they live on and keep on spinning there. The tape is short now, just a tiny fraction of what it was originally, but memory is like that. It overlays voices, cuts out what is inessential, replenishes their fading sense, and implacably replays, over and over again, the bits that one might be happiest to delete.

Then there are the silences between the words. I care for those silences least of all. Because the silences are never complete. They are full of murmurs, characteristic flutters, sighs, groans. The real sounds of an imprisoned man. How many shades of sigh exist, for example? Only these spools know. Consider me mad, but as I say: I find these silences the most difficult to bear.

"Do you hate me, Enrique?"

"Of course I hate you, Dad. Do you want some water? I've still got a bit . . . Don't drink it all, though."

Gulping, long, heavy gulping. Silence. A creaking, the creaking of a wire mattress. Even in imprisonment a man will seek to make himself comfortable. I have become sensitive to that nowadays, highly sensitive. Groans.

"Do you need a hand, Dad?"

"No, it's okay now."

"Does it hurt?"

"It's okay now. I wanted what was best for you, Enrique. You didn't know what you wanted . . . You couldn't have known. You had to live, that was my only purpose . . . to win time, to survive."

"I hope they kill us."

"Don't talk such nonsense, Enrique! They have no real evidence. We did nothing. They'll have to release us!"

"I no longer want to get out of here. They have to do me that one favor. They may even do it, what's more, as they don't know that they'd be doing me a favor."

"You're raving, Enrique! Think about life! Think about the world!"

"I can't. You turned the world upside down for me, Dad. If they don't kill me, I'll become a murderer. And it could be that you will be first, Dad . . . You want some water? More water?"

The spool spins, my memory is chock-full of sounds.

"Is it evening yet, Enrique?"

"Probably, Dad. Beyond these walls, right now, people are saying 'Good evening, ma'am. Good evening, sir. Nice evening we're having. And how's the family?' "

"Have you any idea, Enrique, what an evening on the outside is really like? A simple everyday evening . . . when the city lights suddenly come on . . . Simple, familiar lights that offer aperitifs, refreshments, trendy and durable goods. The smells, Enrique—petrol, sweat, cologne. The sounds . . ."

"Don't fantasize, Dad. We're going to die before too long!"

"No. Enrique! No! My friends can't leave me in the lurch. My death would cast a shadow on them too, a massive shadow. No, there's no way they'd be able to tolerate that . . . I wouldn't tolerate it either, if I were a big businessman on the outside, a leading businessman . . . No, it's not possible! Even now your mother will be leaving no stone unturned out there . . . throwing every contact onto the scales. Commerce is the state's raison d'être, is that clear? Even the Colonel has to bow down before commerce!"

"You amaze me, Dad! You're still living in hope, even now? But what do you want? What can you still want, after everything that has happened?"

Now there was a sound. A word that I didn't understand. I had to double the volume to make out the whisper. And even though I am unable to share in it, now that my own future has become decidedly dubious, I'm coming round to an understanding of the rapture that Salinas distilled into this one word:

"Life."

Then one day the atrocity took place. You will undoubtedly recall it. How could you not! There was a huge commotion: a combing of the scene, a state of alert, and whatnot. Cabinet sessions, a parliamentary commission, a diplomatic scandal, international protests. For a few days the whole world yammered about nothing else.

And the Colonel graced our office with a visit.

"Bloody fools! What are you wasting your time on here?" For five minutes he unleashed a torrent of anger on us, and we could only cringe with bowed heads, like plants in a downpour. Then he slowly calmed down, rather like a passing thunderstorm.

"What's happened in the Salinas case?" he suddenly asked—not directing the question at Diaz, at Rodriguez, or at even me, but tossing it up in the air like a ball, for whoever fielded it.

No one reached out to catch it, so I, the new boy, fielded it.

"For the time being," I say, "we're at a dead end."

"Hmm," the Colonel mused. "A dead end. And what am I supposed to understand by that?" he asked me in none too friendly a manner.

"At present," I say, "our inquiries have thingy . . . run out of leads."

"Hmm. So, what do you propose be done?" A nasty question, that, and extremely hazardous. I could have said very cagily that Diaz was the only one who had the authority to make a suggestion here. Out of the corner of my eye I picked up Diaz's inimitable smile and the leopard glower of Rodriguez's smoldering eyes. But I had caught the ball, and now that I had caught it, I was going to run with it.

"We ought to set them free." This time I didn't even stutter.

"Hmm. And what condition are they in?" the Colonel asked.

At that point there was silence, to be sure, a big silence.

"Hmm." The Colonel's voice gradually grew louder,

more highly pitched and threatening, like a siren. "So my Corps is holding innocent people prisoner. My Corps is grilling innocent people. My Corps is torturing innocent people. What am I to say to parliament? What am I to say to the chamber of commerce? What am I to say to the foreign press?"

By now he was standing in front of me and yelling at my face:

"Inspector, I'm holding you personally responsible for this! I'm holding you responsible! I'll have you sentenced and locked away to rot in prison! Do you understand?!"

I understood all right, you bet I did. I understood well enough to be quaking in my boots. But it was not due to the Colonel that I was quaking, though you might well think so. At that moment I was quaking due to the logic, and nothing else.

Then all at once the Colonel gripped me by the nose, right and proper, between two fingers, the way one does with a young kid. He gave it a few twists, then benevolently made a dismissive gesture.

"You little monkey!" he says affectionately. "You little monkey!"

With that, he stepped over to Rodriguez's desk. The model had caught the Colonel's eye—I had noticed that earlier.

"And what's that?" he inquired.

"That?" Rodriguez cracked a bashful smile. "That's a Boger swing."

"Boger?" It's interesting, but everyone always questions that right away. "Why Boger?"

"He invented it," Rodriguez explained, and launched into a recital of the details. You are familiar with the spiel, and I am loath to repeat it. "This bit here"— he traced a small circle over it with his finger—"is freed up."

He didn't need to say much more; the Colonel soon got the gist.

"Pigs," he said affectionately. "You filthy little piggies." He spun the doll a few times. "Send this Boger to me for a talk."

"We can't do that, Colonel," Diaz apologized.

"Why not?" The Colonel was startled.

"Because he's serving a life sentence in Germany." Yes, that's Diaz for you. He says nothing but meanwhile checks on things, then suddenly brings out a nugget of learning, always when it's awkward for somebody. He makes no exceptions, not even for the Colonel.

"Bloody fools!" The Colonel's brow darkened as he rushed for the exit.

"Colonel!" Diaz tossed after him. "What are we to do in the Salinas case?"

The Colonel turned and pondered for a second.

"Gather your evidence. A summary court will be convened an hour and a half from now."

Not that Diaz needed an hour and a half. I'll be hanged if anyone could have put together as speedily as Diaz a watertight investigational file on conspiracy to engage in criminal acts endangering Homeland security.

Two hours later we were standing in a window bay with Diaz. It was a classical window bay, in one of the Headquarters' classical corridors. It overlooked a narrow courtyard. There was a line of posts on one side. The two Salinases, father and son, were tied up against two posts in the middle. Opposite them were two rows of guards: the firing squad.

"Uncivil." Diaz made a wry face. He was in a gloomy mood; it would sometimes come upon him in his idle moments. "Our line of work is hazardous," he mused. "Today you can be standing up here at the window, but then tomorrow, who knows? You may be down there, tied to a post."

At that moment the fusillade cracked. Did I jump? I don't know. All at once I sensed that Diaz was looking at me.

"Scared?" His smooth face beamed with insolent curiosity. I would have been more than happy to take a swing at him. I already knew then that, when the time came, he would make himself scarce, and it would be futile sending out an APB. He would never be captured. It is always me whom they catch—people like me, I mean.

"Of what?" I asked Diaz.

"Well." He nodded toward the courtyard where the two Salinases were sagging on their fetters like empty sacks. "Of that!"

"That." I shrugged. "I'm not afraid of that. Only the long road that leads to it."

After all, I was still just a new boy then, as I say.